THE
ARCHITECT

A NOVEL

NAWZAD OTHMAN

The Architect

Published by Wheatmark*
2030 East Speedway Boulevard, Suite 106
Tucson, Arizona 85719 USA
www.wheatmark.com

ISBN: 978-1-62787-897-5 (paperback)
ISBN: 978-1-62787-898-2 (ebook)
LCCN: 2021918944

Bulk ordering discounts are available through Wheatmark, Inc. For more information, email orders@wheatmark.com or call 1-888-934-0888.

1

THE MEDICAL EXAMINER completed his autopsy of the man the authorities found shot to death and buried in the desert two kilometers outside of Dubai.

The victim was shot in the back of the head. His hands and feet were tied together with ropes.

A police officer walked in the autopsy room to find out about the identity of the victim. He asked the examiner if he had any preliminary clues.

"He was killed by one shot to the back of the skull," the medical examiner said, pointing at the point of entry. "He is a big man, Caucasian, but I can't tell much more than that until we get the DNA test results. That should tell us much more."

"How about any clues on his clothing or jewelry?" the officer asked.

"Nothing on him. He was stripped clean, except for this photo which we found in the corner of a hidden pocket sewn in his jacket," the examiner said.

He handed the two-inch square photo to the officer.

"He looks European, well groomed. Look at his face and hair, a professional or a businessman," the officer said, looking at the photograph.

"He looks American to me. You know Americans—they have that arrogant look. What do you think, Officer? Maybe you should show it to the captain. He could be someone important," the medical examiner said.

"You're right, I will. Let me know when you get the DNA results," he said.

He turned the photo over and looked at the back. There was a handwritten name: Andy Sykes.

2

MARWAN AHMED MARWAN, chairman of the board of Pinnacle Enterprises, entered the boardroom. He was a tall, elegant, and imposing figure with a slightly graying and perfectly cropped beard. The eight handpicked board members, the who's who in Dubai, stood up and waited for Marwan to sit down before they retook their seats. The chairman was followed by the CEO, Elias Khoury.

The boardroom was quiet, demanding respect. A handpicked mix of exquisite Islamic art covered the walls—the workmanship of artisans from Egypt, Turkey, and other countries. Every detail had been personally approved by the chairman.

"I called for this special meeting to share with you a disturbing call I received from General Masoud, director of Dubai Internal Security," the chairman said in his usual soft, clear voice.

"Apparently, for some unknown reason, our Al Bustan project is a terrorism target. We don't know by whom or why," the chairman said.

The board members were quiet, focused on what they had just heard. A few exchanged looks, others fidgeted in their chairs. Most were still, waiting to hear more.

"Our project is not a secret; it has been widely publicized and planned as our most ambitious. News of it has been well received and eagerly anticipated. It is well known that we intend to use the latest technology to create an exceptional project and probably one of the most secure. Why these threats? We don't know," he said. "Our national security agency has picked up significant online chatter that some groups believe what we are proposing is a threat. Whether these are criminals in pursuit of treasure or they're state-sponsored, we don't know. I hope this can be resolved quickly. I will keep you informed. In the meantime, please stay alert."

The room was quiet.

"Elias, please bring us up to date," he added.

Elias Khoury cleared his throat; he looked the part of the CEO of a major corporation. His graying hair and handsome face were perfectly enhanced by his well-tailored, dark-blue Italian suit. A Lebanese American with an MBA and a law degree from Harvard, Elias had left his position as senior vice president of Global Trading Inc., based in New York, to join Pinnacle Enterprises three years earlier.

"Thank you, Chairman Marwan. We are ready to finalize and sign the contract. The team of architects from STR, the lead company from Los Angeles, should arrive tomorrow night. I intend to give them authorization to proceed," Elias said, making eye contact with each board member.

"The work includes the latest defensive cyber capabilities, driven by CTC—Cyber Technologies Corporation, an American cybersecurity company based in Boston," he went on. "To refresh your memory, a year ago our Department of Defense signed a contract with CTC, with the approval and collaboration of the US Department of Defense, to test the latest cyber defense measure."

Elias looked at his notes, then continued.

"CTC is one of the leading security companies in the world. They work with governments, major organizations, and international companies to put in place software and security measures against hackers' malware and ransomware. We hired them a year ago to remove the ransomware from our building, where hackers had penetrated our electrical and HVAC systems, demanding ransom.

CTC was successful in removing the ransomware without paying any ransom."

He took a sip of water.

"What is planned for Al Bustan requires approval from the US for licensing sophisticated technology for commercial applications in foreign countries," Elias said. "CTC has developed a new method of defense that they propose for our project. It is not software, the standard for combating hackers, but hardware, new and still classified. Their work with our Department of Defense has been promising but limited. What is being proposed is to test the hardware on a much larger building—our tower in Al Bustan."

"Can they do that? This sounds complicated," a board member asked.

"They believe they can achieve that through collaboration with STR architects, the leaders in the application of artificial intelligence," Elias said. "They say it will add the missing ingredient to achieve the breakthrough. Both teams will be here this week. I intend to move the process forward. Both governments are supportive of our project; they are hopeful that we succeed. That would allow CTC, the inventors of the hardware, to apply it as a more efficient and less vulnerable model for security against hackers. The US government approved our request and granted CTC the license."

Elias stopped and looked at the chairman, who nodded his approval. "Thank you, Elias. Please keep us informed. Any questions?" Marwan asked.

"How serious are these concerns of being targeted?" Abdulla Amin, the youngest board member, asked.

"According to General Masoud, they are very serious," Elias replied.

"What is the target? We are just starting the design; there is nothing to attack. Why not target one of our many existing buildings?" the young board member asked, leaning forward.

"That is the mystery. We don't know. Our national security people are puzzled. They continue to monitor and evaluate what they hear. They don't believe that any of us are targeted, but they recommend we stay alert to anything unusual," Elias said.

"You mentioned the architect. How does he fit in with the technology company?" another board member asked.

"The way I understand it, the hardware developed by CTC is advanced microprocessors placed within computers and the servers. The results from their own studies and the work with our Defense Department have been positive. Its application has been limited to protecting individual units and small networks. To expand its reach and protect a much larger network, such as our project, is where the architects come in," Elias said.

"STR, the architecture firm we selected, are leaders in the application of the latest technology in designing mega projects such as Al Bustan. They are specialists in the placement of sensors and microprocessors throughout the building to protect and adjust as needed to physical and climate challenges. This unique capability is planned to be integrated with the new security hardware to create a protective technology wall around the building. With the blessing of the two governments, we are optimistic this will not only work well but could also be a universal prototype." The CEO was visibly excited by the prospect.

"Will the new system be implemented immediately without additional testing?" the young board member asked.

"No. We have an existing building that we own and plan to use as our testing site. The immediate assignment of our new team is to move ahead with the testing while the design of Al Bustan is in process," Elias answered.

The chairman stood up, nodding to board members, before leaving for a speaking engagement at the grand opening of an agricultural project.

After he left, Elias answered more questions from board members about potential security concerns, then he went back to his office and closed the door. He picked up his cell phone and punched in a memorized number.

"I'll see you tomorrow night. I'm concerned about all the noise. Don't forget what I told you," he said.

3

MARY TOBIAS, DIRECTOR of the cybersecurity special team for the CIA, was in her office at headquarters. She needed to talk to General Masoud. He was an old and trusted friend, and from the way he spoke during the previous call, she knew something was up. Earlier in the week, the general had expressed concerns about potential terrorist attacks possibly relating to the Al Bustan project in Dubai. That's when she'd told Natalie, her team leader, to get the project team to check it out.

Until that point, Mary had been focused on the Russians and their state-initiated, or state-tolerated, hacking. Their level of activity, sophistication, and boldness was alarming, and they had stepped up their cyberattacks, penetrating all corners of government, corporations, and infrastructure facilities with impunity.

She knew the Russians could inflict significant harm on the US economy without firing a single shot, considering how far they had succeeded in interfering with the elections. Now that the Chinese and the Iranians were also upping their game, urgent countermeasures had to be implemented. Her team must deliver, and she knew she'd push them hard. Mary picked up her phone and dialed a number; the secure line connected her directly to General Pitman in the Pentagon. Looking out her office window at the sun glinting on all the cars in the parking lot below, she explained the Dubai project and asked if he knew anything about it. Pitman said he didn't but would check around and get back to her. When he put the phone down, she knew she'd ruined his day.

As she hung up, the phone rang; it was General Masoud.

"Hello, General," Mary said.

"Hello, Mary. Following up on our earlier conversation, we have been hearing more chatter about the Al Bustan project. We keep hearing that some entities, most probably state-sponsored, may be targeting this project."

"That doesn't tell me anything. Why would they target a project that has not yet started? I haven't heard of any plans by us that would make this development a target," Mary said.

"There aren't. But the Al Bustan development is planned to be one of the most advanced building projects in the use of technology. For some reason, the new cyber technology has become suspect," the general replied.

"How is that a threat?" Mary asked.

"We don't know. We have an agreement with the developer to install the advanced cyber defense system within the project to be used as a prototype for other commercial buildings. What is bothering me is the target. We believe the American team may be the target," he said.

"What team?" Mary said, surprised.

"The lead architects and security specialists; both teams are Americans."

"If that's true, this is serious. Why do you think they are the targets?"

"I am assuming it is to send us a message to abort the project since there is nothing physical to attack" he said.

"Masoud, I know you have a sophisticated monitoring security system in place. Have you been able to track the chatter?" Mary asked.

"That is the puzzle. We have not. They have to be a highly skilled group to be able to evade us. Mary, check around on your end, please. Maybe there is something about this hardware we are missing," Masoud said.

"I'm meeting with our deputy director soon. I'll let you know what I find out."

"Okay, Mary. Stay well." He ended the call.

Mary took the elevator to the third floor and started walking slowly toward the office of Tim Patterson, the deputy director of the CIA. Mary, a fifty-year-old, fit, slightly graying twenty-five-year veteran of the CIA, was not a fan of the deputy director. She was a friend of the director, who trained her, but she understood and respected the chain of command.

She stopped at the door, counted to ten, took a deep breath, and walked in. Tim Patterson was sitting in his red leather chair behind a huge mahogany desk and looking at the three twenty-four-inch computer screens. The walls were covered with photographs of him with important people in a variety of venues: playing golf, watching a ball game, or standing with high-ranking officials. Three television screens dominated one wall.

When he waved for Mary to come in and have a seat, his West Point ring and Rolex watch glittered in the light.

"Mary, we need you to go to Dubai," he said as soon as she sat.

"Dubai . . . what for?" Mary's hands pressed hard on her chair; she felt her knuckles turning white.

"The Al Bustan project. Our UAE partners are concerned about a terrorist attack," he said.

"Yes, I heard. General Masoud called and shared that with me. But what does that have to do with me and my team? We're chasing hackers and bad actors through cyberspace. Chasing terrorists is not our mission. I told General Masoud that. Did you tell him you will be sending me?" Mary's face was turning red as her eyes laser-focused on him.

"No, I did not. He asked for you."

"And what did you say? 'Oh, yes, of course, she has nothing to do.'" Her cheeks were bright red now.

"Mary, you know better. I told him how busy you are. You know what he said? He said you are the only person he wanted to work with." He sounded a bit smug, Mary thought.

"Besides, our director is paying close attention to this. He received the call from the defense minister. This project has their attention. They supported it, and they want it to succeed. They absolutely do not want anything to get in the way."

"Alright, Tim, I get it. How soon do you want me there?" Mary asked.

"Right away. Take the plane tomorrow."

"Okay. I'll let General Masoud know. I will take Natalie and Rusty with me. They're waiting for me in my office. I asked them to give me a briefing on the project, a favor for General Masoud. Anything else?"

"No, but keep me informed," Tim replied.

Mary got up, turned around, and walked out.

4

THE TEAM WAS waiting in Mary's office. Natalie Arseniev was standing on the right with a file in her hands. A graduate from MIT with a degree in mathematics, she was a tall and athletic-looking blonde, wearing jeans and a beige blouse. She moved nimbly, like an athlete, to greet Mary. She had cowboy boots on, a pair she bought when she was in Dallas on an assignment.

Rusty Crawly, the technology guru, was sitting in a chair on the left side of Mary's desk. He was reading the report he had prepared for the meeting. He was short and stocky, perfectly built for a varsity wrestler at Ohio State.

"Hi, Mary, how did it go with our lovely leader?" Natalie said, smiling.

"Well, we are leaving for Dubai tomorrow. Tell me what you have found," Mary said.

"Wait, did I hear you right: we are flying to Dubai tomorrow?" Natalie asked.

"Yes, that's right. Pack tonight; we leave at three in the afternoon. They have a plane ready for us, all preplanned. So, now, back to what you found."

"Interesting stuff," Rusty said.

"We connected with our people in the region. The Al Bustan project is the largest since Burj Khalifa, the world's tallest building.

Their assessment is that the project is real; the developer, Pinnacle Enterprises, is one of the premier and most highly respected companies in Dubai. They have selected an international team led by STR, an architecture firm in Los Angeles that is to design and manage the project. CTC—Cyber Technologies Corporation from Boston—is leading the security effort," Natalie said.

"CTC? That's the company our national security advisor came from. He was their former CEO," Mary said.

"Yes, that is right," Rusty said.

"This is another iconic project in Dubai. What may be attracting the bad guys is its cybersecurity plan. The short version is the introduction to and placement of new and, for now, classified hardware in the project. Several months ago, with our approval, the UAE Ministry of Defense contracted with CTC to test the hardware in one of the defense department facilities. According to our Department of Defense, the results have been positive," Rusty added.

"I know. What I need to understand is this new hardware. What is it? How does it work? And why this attention?" Mary flipped through the brief files her team prepared for her.

"Mary, I did some research," Natalie started, still standing with the folder in her hand. "For years, we have known that software alone cannot contain or totally defend against hackers, spyware, malware, or ransomware. Many hackers are sophisticated programmers and technical cyber specialists, always probing and discovering new ways to penetrate our systems. No one is safe. No government agency, corporation, or utility company is safe. We fight them with the technical means we have, but they find new ways to get around our defenses," Natalie said. She removed a sheet from her folder and looked at it.

"For the last few years, a number of our giant technology companies have been working on hardware that supports our software capabilities or as a standalone defense system. DARPA, the Defense

Advanced Research Projects Agency, has funded a number of research projects to develop this kind of hardware." Natalie looked at her notes again and then nodded at Rusty.

"A quick history: DARPA was established by Congress in the fifties. Its mission was straightforward: we will stay ahead of other countries in our innovations and advanced technologies. They worked in collaboration with the private sector, funding the research and contracting with our best scientists and engineers. Many of our technical breakthroughs come from that collaboration. The CTC's new hardware, we believe, is a product of that collaboration," Rusty added.

"The testing of the new hardware has so far been promising, according to the Department of Defense. The testing, however, has been limited to individual computers through new microprocessors. They have also tested the hardware in a new server for small networks, and the outcome, we understand, has also been positive. All the testing by the CTC was done for both the DoD and for major corporations," Natalie said.

"So far, that is all good news. What does Dubai have to do with any of this?" Mary asked.

"Here's where it gets a bit unclear. Six months ago, CTC, which has been working on cybersecurity in the UAE for several years, convinced the UAE government and the US DoD to test the new hardware on a larger network in one of the UAE Department of Defense facilities. The ministry could not or would not provide the right building. So, CTC convinced our DoD to give them the clearance and the licensing needed for the installation and testing of the hardware in a commercial building. That's where Al Bustan comes in," Natalie explained.

"What is the hardware?" Mary asked.

"It is an advanced and sophisticated server connected to a small network. It protects the network against unwanted interference by creating a cyber wall around the network. The results from the UAE are positive and promising," Natalie said. "Based on those results, CTC convinced the developer and both governments to place a new, more advanced server in the mega tower in the Al Bustan project to test it on a much larger network: the tower."

"That's where STR, the American firm, comes in. They are the specialists in the use of technology in tall buildings. They have mastered the placement of censors and microprocessors in the building skin and key interior locations that can provide the capabilities to adjust to external conditions.

The CTC believes that collaboration with the architects should produce the desired result: the new server can protect the networks for the entire building," Rusty said.

"Does our defense department believe it will work? It's a game changer if it does," Mary asked.

"From what we hear, they do. At least they're hoping it does. There are some within the department who are skeptical. There are also some concerns that the department has given CTC too much freedom in directing this initiative in a foreign country," Natalie said.

"A foreign country that is a strong ally. How about the developer, Pinnacle Enterprises? Aren't they taking a huge risk if this does not work?" Mary asked.

"From what we hear, the answer is no. They are operating on the assumption they move forward as traditionally planned, while the new cybersecurity hardware for the building is being tested." Natalie answered.

"Why this sudden noise about a terrorist threat?" Mary asked, looking at the reports.

"Another puzzle. It came out of nowhere; we don't know why or by whom. It does not add up. What is being planned is a server, albeit a special, state-of-the-art, advanced piece of hardware, but it is still a server that is used as an effective protection against cyberattacks. As far as we know, it is not a threat or an offensive weapon by any measure," Natalie replied, checking her notes.

"So why this false assumption out there? The only explanation I can come up with is the misinformation is spread deliberately. But why? Hundreds of iconic buildings have been built in Dubai without incident. Al Bustan, for some reason, is getting all this wrong attention. We need to find out who is behind this. It simply can't be this new hardware, this server." Natalie placed her file down on Mary's desk.

Mary knew how analytical Natalie was. She leaned back, looked at her two team members, and stayed quiet for quite a long time.

"I get the picture. So why do you think we are going to Dubai?" Mary said, as if asking herself the question. When neither answered, she stated.

"There's more to the story than we realize. I want you two to dig into this: find out if there is any more to this hardware and how it was approved by DoD. In the meantime, I'll talk with General Masoud and let him know that we will be arriving in Dubai."

Rusty and Natalie picked up their folders and left. Mary sat still in her chair, picked up the rubber ball on her desk, and started squeezing, deep in thought—a habit she had as long as she could remember. She picked up the phone to call the director of the CIA, hesitated, and then placed the phone down.

She got up ready to leave when her phone rang. She picked it up. It was General Masoud.

"Mary, we have a situation. A young Bedouin found a body in the desert, close to Dubai and contacted us. The victim appeared to be Caucasian. There was nothing on him to identify him except for a photo with a name on the back of the photo. We checked and found out that the person in the photo is the lead architect from Los Angeles, whose firm has been awarded the Al Bustan project. He is scheduled to arrive in Dubai tomorrow night," the general said.

"Masoud, this is troubling. Is the architect the target?" Mary asked.

"We don't know yet," Masoud said.

"Any clues about the victim's identity?"

"Not yet, but we should know soon."

"What is the name of the architect?" Mary said.

"Andy Sykes," the General said.

5

EMIRATES AIRLINES BUSINESS class was comfortable. The direct flight from LAX to Dubai was over fifteen hours, and as always, Andy Sykes, the lead STR architect and project manager for the Al Bustan project in Dubai, was wearing sweats.

Once in the air and feeling relaxed, he was reflective about how quickly the events unfolded and the Herculean effort it had taken to put the team together, write the proposal, and prepare for the interview; it was almost overwhelming.

He was thinking about the team he selected. The team, considered to be the best of the best, included architects, engineers, biologists, and technology and AI specialists from various international companies. This was not an ordinary project, Andy thought. It was about planning and designing a community where all its structures and surrounding landscape are alive, secure, and sustainable. STR expertise and experience in the application of AI were essential and invaluable.

He knew that the most significant technical and the most challenging aspect of the project was the application of advanced technology to cybersecurity in a way that had not been done before—the introduction of a new type of hardware to the project.

Andy Sykes had concerns as to how this could be accomplished having security specialists on the team with whom they had not worked before. Andy was not sure if they really had the special skills they claimed to have.

Adding to his anxiety was the involvement of the US and UAE security agencies. He was particularly unsure of CTC. It was CTC that had recommended Andy and his firm. It was obvious they were connected, but Andy was not sure if they could be trusted or controlled. He had insisted that all the work by CTC had to be approved by Andy and his STR architects. He had placed language to that effect in the proposal. Andy ordered a glass of champagne from the tall, dark-haired European flight attendant. As the 380 airbus reached the flight altitude, he took out his notebook and started writing. It was his habit to write down his thoughts.

Andy wished his father was still alive to share this moment. He always remembered his dad's words: "Andy, you can accomplish great things if you truly believe and are passionate about whatever you do. You are just wasting time, running around with your camera taking pictures or playing with your computer. Now you want to enroll in art classes. Where is that going to get you?"

Well, in the end, it was his mother's encouragement that helped him. She not only rescued him from his father but also from himself. She encouraged him to become an architect. "That is art, right?" she would say.

Andy's passions were science and math. Computer science was very appealing. He was also drawn to architecture. He listened to his mother and enrolled in UC Berkeley's architecture school and took as many math and computer science classes as possible. He never looked back and graduated with a dual degree in architecture and computer science.

After adjusting his seat, he removed the thick proposal from his fifteen-year-old stained and frayed backpack. He had read and reread his winning proposal so many times that he had almost memorized it. He wanted to be ready for the discussions with the client.

After dinner, a walk back to the full bar and lounge on the plane, a night cap, and small talk, Andy returned to his seat. The bed had already been made for him for a comfortable sleep.

———

Once the plane landed hours later, going through customs in Dubai was smooth and uneventful. Andy always wondered why they couldn't do that back in the States. As always, he only had a carry-on bag. He left the airport in a cab toward Jumeirah Beach Hotel, where he had stayed before and loved it.

———

Andy did not notice the young man following him from the airport, who got in a taxi and directed the driver to follow Andy's taxi. He was not a native Emirati; he looked like one of thousands of expats from all over the world on the hunt for business.

After Andy arrived at the hotel, the young man pulled out his cell phone and punched in some numbers. He said, "Yes, he is here" and then listened for his instructions. He hung up, left the cab, and casually walked in the hotel.

———

Andy checked in and took the elevator to his junior suite with a spectacular view of the city. He unpacked, took a hot shower, and got dressed for the evening. He was to meet Ayman Nouri, a local architect and part of the team; it was 9:00 p.m.

Ayman was waiting for him in the lobby for dinner and a review of the next day's schedule. A Jordanian American, Ayman obtained his architectural degree from the American University in Beirut (AUB) with a masters from the University of Pennsylvania.

He was the owner of the local firm in Dubai collaborating with STR. Ayman, a bilingual, articulate, and highly connected member of the team, was a great find for STR, helpful in navigating the business culture and the dos and don'ts. He was a handsome man, well dressed with high energy, and was very fit. He had a presence that demanded attention and respect, and he was always animated, full of energy and enthusiasm.

They immediately went to the Lebanese restaurant in the hotel. After a few sips of arak and some mezza to start with, the two were relaxed, ready for a fabulous dinner and review of the next day's agenda. Ayman laid out the itinerary. He told Andy that finalizing the agreement required patience and finesse. He warned him that the proposal, already detailed and accepted, would still be challenged: the fees were too high, and the timeframe to complete the project was too long.

"Remember, the client likes you and wants you. Don't try to reach a final agreement the first day. In fact, you may not reach an agreement until the day you are planning to leave. Typically, we will meet socially and have a few dinners. They want to check you out further. I will be with you the whole time," Ayman told Andy.

Andy was so thankful to have Ayman by his side. He had been through tough negotiations before, but this was different; this was the major league, the global arena, and Andy was ready.

They were scheduled to meet with the client the next morning at ten. Ayman was going to pick him up at nine thirty. Andy said goodnight to Ayman and took the elevator to his room.

———

Ayman left the hotel, got into his silver Porsche SUV, and drove away. He did not go home. He drove to the old part of Dubai with its traditional architecture and old souks. He parked the car in front of an old café and went inside.

He went straight to a room in the back, opened the door, and walked in. Inside was one person, an older man, sitting behind a huge desk. He was intently looking at his computer. He turned and smiled as Ayman walked in and waved to him to sit down.

"Marhaba Ayman, good to see you. I hope all is well with you and your family," the older man said.

"Yes, it is, Abu Haider. All is well, thank you," Ayman replied.

"What do you think about the architect Andy Sykes? You met with him tonight. What are your thoughts? Is he as capable as we are told? Tell me about the company. Was the right team selected?" the old man asked.

"I did my research before I agreed to be part of their team," Ayman said.

"The two key principles of the firm are Bob Thornton and John Schneider, who is the founder. The two have different but complementary visions for the direction of the firm. John Schneider is a purist, a traditional architect. He has a national reputation for great design, has won numerous national and international awards, lectured extensively, and taught classes in architecture schools. He has a reputation for integrity and an uncompromising commitment to design excellence. He started the firm thirty years earlier and brought in Bob Thornton and Paul Rataki as partners," Ayman said.

"Bob Thornton is the new breed of architect, heavy reliance on technology. He is convinced that the future of architecture is driven by AI. He created the technology and AI department for the firm," Ayman continued.

"That is good Ayman, very good. I like that, the traditional and the modern," the older man said.

"Andy Sykes is the driver of the initiative. He shares the same vision as Bob. Both know the decision by Pinnacle Enterprises to hire them was heavily influenced by their commitment to the integration of AI to their practice.

"They are the specialists in that field. Dubai is the perfect place to give them the opportunity to expand and demonstrate their capabilities and our Al Bustan project is the ideal project for their skills," Ayman said.

"The architect, Andy Sykes, do you like him?" the older man asked, as he stood up, came around the desk, and leaned on his cane.

"I like him, and I believe he is very capable. In my opinion, he is one of only a handful of experts anywhere who has this kind of knowledge and skill for the new construction," Ayman replied.

"Stay close to him, Ayman. I want to know everything about the project details, specifically the cybersecurity. We have to be certain there are no hidden plans. Keep me informed," the older man said.

"I will, sir," Ayman replied.

"How about CTC? Have you met with any of them yet?" the older man asked.

"No, sir, not yet. We should this week," Ayman replied, as he stood up, ready to leave the room.

"One more thing Ayman. This whole business about a potential terrorist attack is strange. Something about it bothers me. It is not logical. Have you heard anything? Do you have any thoughts?" the old man asked.

"I feel the same way you do, sir—too many questions and no simple answers. The only thing in my opinion that may lead to answers is the new server. It has to be," Ayman said and left the room.

6

ANDY GOT BACK to his room and immediately called his wife, Jennifer. It was 11:00 a.m. LA time. He told her the trip was fine, he had a great dinner with Ayman, and he was ready for a good night's sleep. The next day would be a big one. Both agreed that she would travel with him on the next trip once the contract was signed.

Jennifer Robinson Sykes was a lawyer who worked for a mid-sized firm in Los Angeles; her work focused on international human rights and immigration issues. She and Andy were married for five years and had no children. They met at a fundraiser, felt instant attraction, and were never apart since then. They had much in common, especially love of the outdoors, hiking, biking, fly fishing, and travel. They were soulmates.

Jennifer was born and raised in a small town in the state of Washington. Both her parents were teachers. After getting a degree in history from the University of Washington in Seattle, she spent two years with the Peace Corps stationed in Cameroon, Africa, an experience she loved and would never forget. After the Peace Corps, she went back to the University of Washington for her law degree.

After his call with his wife, Andy called Bob Thornton, his boss, who was in his office.

"Bob, I had a great dinner with Ayman, our local team member. I wish you were here with us. We are lucky to have him with us. He is a great help. Tomorrow is our meeting with the client; hopefully we can finalize our agreement," Andy said.

"I'm sorry Andy for sending you to Dubai alone to finalize a contract. I should be there with you. I'm still puzzled about why they insisted that for this first round you come accompanied only by Ayman Nouri and the representative of CTC," Bob said.

"They said they only wanted to meet with the technical team to start with. No idea why," Andy said. Bob demanded that Andy report the progress often and make no commitments without his approval.

"I had a long chat with John Schneider, our managing partner, who suggested that I join you in Dubai for support," Bob said. "I'll leave within two days and meet you there. In the meantime, I'm expecting to see Tyler Grant."

"I hope this is it. He'll accept our offer. We need him," Andy said.

"I agree. We need his experience on US embassies and national security clearances," Bob said.

"Remember, he was highly recommended by CTC," Andy said.

———

Bob and Andy hung up, and a few minutes later, Tyler Grant arrived in Bob's office. He was forty-two, tall, and athletic-looking with nervous energy; he came across as a man on a mission, in a hurry. His credentials as an architect were impressive. His body of work was remarkable.

Tyler sat down across from Bob; he was relaxed with a bottle of water in his hand, taking periodic sips. He asked Bob where Andy was. Bob told him. Tyler was surprised that Bob, as the principal in charge of this massive project, was not there with him. Bob told him he would be leaving to join Andy the next day.

Bob looked at Tyler, waiting for a sign. He watched him drinking from his water bottle, and appeared to be relaxed. *A good sign,* Bob thought.

"Tyler, let me say it again. We at STR want you to join us. As I have told you so many times, you would be a great addition to this firm. Andy wants you; John Schneider, our managing partner, and other principals want you. We all feel that you share our vision. I hope—we all hope—that you have decided to join us," Bob said, leaning forward toward Tyler.

Tyler placed the water bottle on the coffee table and also leaned forward. "Bob, I have given this a lot of thought and have decided to accept your offer. I am excited to join you; you are so right about the vision and direction you have laid out for STR. I am in. Your compensation package and benefits are generous. Thank you. However, I do have some conditions. It is more of a clarification of what we have discussed before."

"That is just great, Tyler. You made my day." Bob stood up and shook Tyler's hand. "Now explain to me exactly what your conditions are."

"The design team has to move to Dubai for the duration. You open a Dubai office. I lead the design team for this project and this project only for the duration. You hire an office manager to take care of the administration of the office. I report only to Andy. I manage all technology and AI specialists. That's it."

Bob was delighted with the terms. They had already made the decision to open an office in Dubai, a project office to begin with. "Tyler, I accept. Welcome to STR. You are aware that we have not yet signed the contract, but we are confident this will happen soon. We should have it within a week or two. As I said, I'm flying to Dubai tomorrow. In the meantime, I will let John and Andy know about you accepting our offer. When can I announce it?"

"Bob, I have already resigned. I can formally join you in two weeks. Announce it today if you wish. I have to run back to the office to take care of a few details with my current projects and hand off to others." Bob and Tyler were both standing. After another hand-shake, Tyler left.

Bob immediately emailed Andy and John Schneider and told them the good news.

———

It was time to celebrate; he was feeling energized. He picked up the phone and called Sally to see if she would join him for dinner at the hotel restaurant, a night together before he left for Dubai the next day. Sally laughed as this was the same night of the week they had been spending together for months.

He had a resident apartment at the hotel where he spent many nights rather than making the long drive home, especially when work demanded late nights to meet deadlines. He was divorced. It had been two years since he met Sally. She was the free spirit he needed and loved. He rushed out of the office and headed to his hotel apartment.

Sally was already in the apartment when he got there; she had a key. She jumped up and leaped toward Bob with her arms around him. He held on to her, joyful and passionate. He kissed her on the lips, her eyes, and cheeks. Sally held Bob's hand and looked at him with her piercing eyes. "Bob, you should be excited. This is a huge win for you and the firm, but you appear distracted. Is something bothering you?"

"I'm not sure if I am overwhelmed with excitement, or it's just my tendency to worry," he replied after a long pause.

"Worry about what? You crazy man, you should be jumping up and down and celebrating your win."

"An alarm bell in my gut. I can't help it. I am a chronic wor-rier. But you are right; it is time to celebrate." Bob grabbed Sally—a petite, elegant, dark-haired, and beautiful woman—lifted her up in his arms, and carried her to the king-size bed.

7

THE CORPORATE GULF Stream G650ER flying from Boston to Dubai had only two passengers: Bill Sorenson, executive VP of CTC, and Jason Bower, the technical director. Bill, in his late fifties, placed the file he was reading down on the table and picked up his glass, half full of Johnny Walker Blue Label, his third.

Jason was watching Bill put away the alcohol; it was no secret within the company about Bill's drinking. Jason, the forty-two-year-old marathoner, finished his beer, stood up, and walked to the restroom. When he came back, the hostess had placed another glass of scotch on Bill's tray.

"We will be landing shortly; our car will be waiting for us. I'll drop you off at the hotel and place the two boxes in the designated secure areas. Tonight, we'll be meeting in the private room at the Buddha Bar for dinner. Our friend will join us there," Bill said.

"I can go with you to place the two boxes," Jason said.

"No, that is not necessary," Bill stated, trying to end the conversation.

"Bill, you asked me to keep one of the boxes in my place in Boston for safekeeping. I took a risk by having that sensitive, highly sophisticated hardware in my house and didn't ask any questions. Now we're heading to Dubai, and you can't tell me what you're doing? What is going on? Why two servers? If I am part of this team, I demand to know." Jason leaned over, glaring at Bill.

Bill did not answer; he picked up his glass and drank the rest of his scotch. His eyes red, he leaned back, avoiding Jason's glare, and slurred, "Jason, I will share with you why the two boxes, I promise. I will this evening at the hotel."

Jason kept staring at Bill but didn't say anything.

A black Cadillac SUV with a driver was waiting for them when the plane landed at Dubai International Airport. Bill and Jason came down the steps, and the driver and a crew member brought down the two suitcases and a crate containing the two boxes and placed them in the SUV. Bill instructed the driver to go to the hotel and drop Jason off first. Farouk Khan, the Pakistani SUV driver who had been Bill's personal driver, assistant, and confidante for years, did not say anything. He just nodded.

When they arrived at the hotel, the Grosvenor House, Jason told Bill he would meet him in the lobby later and that they'd walk together to the Buddha Bar next door. He stepped out of the car, checked in, and went up to his room, where he unpacked and took a quick shower before getting dressed for the evening.

He picked up his secure mobile phone and punched in some numbers, starting with a Washington, DC, area code. The voice on the other end answered immediately. Jason told him about their plans for the evening and that Bill had two boxes to be placed somewhere safe that he did not share with him. Jason said he'd call back with an update later that night after the dinner meeting. They signed off, and he took the elevator to the lobby to meet Bill.

They met at the bar located in the lobby, and each ordered a drink: a scotch for Bill and a Pilsner for Jason. Bill did not explain why he did not take Jason with him to put the boxes in a secure place. Jason did not ask.

After the drink, they walked along the Dubai canal to the Buddha Bar. The famous bar/restaurant was humming with the sound of the crowd and the music. The hostess welcomed them and led them to a private room. Bill told her they were expecting their guest to arrive soon and to bring him to the room.

"Jason, I didn't share where I have stored the two boxes but not because of any trust issue. I simply did not want to place you in a compromising position," Bill said when the hostess left.

"That's fine, Bill. What I still don't understand is why you made a duplicate of the black box server. It doesn't make sense. These are extremely sophisticated and advanced servers; you are jeopardizing the integrity of the initiative for this added risk, not to mention the national security violation. Do you have approval?" Jason was laser focused on Bill.

Bill started fidgeting, moving a spoon around on the table. He avoided Jason's stare. He didn't reply right away but kept staring away into some void, his face a blank.

"Jason, I don't want you involved in this. What I am doing is authorized by higher-ups. It does not violate any national security. The servers are not identical. There is a subtle difference; one is more advanced. We have two in case one does not give us the desired results. I am not sure this is the best approach; the plan was formulated and directed by others. Keeping it quiet is simply to ensure that the plan is not misinterpreted," Bill said, still fidgeting with the spoon.

Just as Jason was about to reply, the hostess came in the room followed by Elias Khoury, CEO of Pinnacle Enterprises. When the hostess left, Elias greeted Bill and Jason with a warm handshake.

"Bill, I don't have enough time to have dinner with you and Jason. I just wanted to make sure the plans are in place and there are no problems," Elias said in his usual relaxed but firm manner.

"Yes, we are on track. I have the server. As soon as you tell us which building to use for testing the system, I will work with the architect to get that phase moving immediately. I understand he is already here. I will connect with him tomorrow morning," Bill said.

"Good. He is coming to the office in the morning to go over the contract. I want you to join us so we are clear on the scope of the work. It will be at ten. Remember, the architects were insistent that your work is done under their supervision and approval. Is that a problem?" Elias asked.

"No, Elias, that will not be a problem. I know how to work with them. I will be there tomorrow morning."

"Before I leave, I need to be very clear that Al Bustan is our most important project. This new hardware, the cybersecurity server, is secondary. We agreed to have it included because of the recommendation of our Defense Ministry and you convincing us of its reliability. But we cannot allow this experimental hardware to get in the way or delay our project. I am sticking my neck out by promoting this hardware and this cyber-security plan." Elias said, still standing.

"Elias, be assured that we have absolute confidence that it will test just fine and will perform as a hardened cyber defense." Bill was back to his confident self again.

"One more thing: our national security agency alerted us that our project may be targeted for some unknown reason, specifically branding our security plan as an American plant for harm. No one knows why or from whom this sudden chatter has erupted. Be aware, and keep me informed if you see or hear anything unusual," Elias said. He shook their hands and left.

"Bill, why didn't you tell him you have two boxes?" Jason asked.

"No one here needs to know beyond the two of us. It will raise too many questions that we don't need right now. I simply want to be sure I have it in case of a capacity issue," Bill replied.

Jason just watched as Bill drained what remained in his glass, his level of anxiety growing.

8

AYMAN PICKED ANDY up at 9:30 a.m. as planned. They headed to the corporate headquarters of Pinnacle Enterprises. Their office on Sheikh Zayed Road was in a sixty-eight-floor imposing but elegant office building with retail and restaurants on the lower four floors. Pinnacle Enterprises occupied the top five.

A company representative met them in the lobby and accompanied them to the sixty-fifth floor. The reception area was decorated with exceptional taste, contemporary elegance mixed with exquisite Islamic art. They were guided to a conference room with a large table in the middle that could seat thirty. There were four people in the room. They rose as Andy and Ayman entered.

Elias Khoury, whom Andy had met during the interviews, warmly greeted them.

"Andy, welcome back to Dubai. Wonderful to see you again. Ayman, welcome. Let me introduce you to our team. Joseph Ferguson is our technical director, in charge of coordinating the design and construction of our projects. Joe has been with us for five years, an engineer educated and trained in England. He is our Englishman. Mounir Al Misri is our financial director in charge of contracts, procurement, and payments, and of course you know Bill Sorenson from CTC. Please be seated," Elias said.

The tea server came in the room and waited. Elias offered coffee, tea, and water to his guests. All three requested Turkish coffee and water. The man left the room and was back within minutes with the orders.

"Our apologies for changing the schedule, Andy. I hope it did not create any inconvenience," Elias stated.

"None at all. In fact, it gave me a chance to visit the project site again," replied Andy.

"Excellent. Let me start by saying the selection process was difficult. We were fortunate to have three extraordinary international teams as finalists. All three of you, in our judgment, were capable of doing the work. The other two finalists were known to us. They have worked on projects for us. All three of you had the right mix of international specialists and local support teams. I have to tell you, though," Elias continued, "your team was unknown to us. We only knew your reputation. Coming to the interview, you were in third place. Andy, you and your team won the project in the interview."

Andy smiled and started to reply. "Mr. Khoury—"

"Please call me Elias," he said.

"Okay. Thank you, Elias. We are very excited and honored that you selected us. We spent an enormous amount of time researching the project needs and selecting the team to deliver for you. I have a message from our senior management in Los Angeles expressing their sincere thanks, and they wanted me to assure you that we are fully committed to providing the needed resources to get the job done. We intend to open an office in Dubai as soon as we sign the agreement. We want our team to be in close coordination with your office," Andy said.

"Andy, did Ayman warn you that we will beat you up on your fees?" Elias smiled.

"Well, yes, he did," Andy replied, also smiling.

Ayman objected. "I said 'slightly' beat you up." They all laughed.

"Andy," the CEO continued, "our plan for you in the next few days is to finalize the agreement and have it signed; in the meantime, we authorize you to start work. You and your team will be paid for this work. What is most important for us is for you to have a clear understanding about our vision and expectations for this project. The first step will be a meeting with our chairman. He is very pleased to have you here. He is expecting us this morning." Elias stood up.

"There is one item I want to make sure we are clear about to include in the agreement," Andy said, still seated.

"What is that, Andy?" Elias asked.

"The cybersecurity plan has to be well defined, both the testing and implementation. I need to understand it and approve the details," Andy said.

"Of course, Andy. I had assumed the two of you have those details worked out," Elias said as he turned around and looked at Bill Sorenson.

"Absolutely, Andy, we can work out the details in the next few days; that was my plan," Bill replied.

Andy looked at Ayman and smiled, relieved. At least for now, it appeared that the project was formally theirs. Negotiating the fees and schedule did not appear to be an issue. The expectations and vision of the chairman was clearly the most important issue.

"Thank you, Elias. I look forward to meeting with the chairman. I am honored and eager to get started. I would also like to share with you how impressed we are with your vision," Andy said.

"Andy," Elias replied, "that is why we selected you. Now that I have both you and Bill here, it is absolutely essential that you get started with testing the new hardware. We cannot have any delays in moving forward with Al Bustan. If the tests do not produce the expected results, the new hardware will not be installed. One more thing: the other eight board members will be in the boardroom with the chairman." Like an accomplished British actor, Elias asked the three members of the winning team to follow him.

The chairman met the group at the entrance of the boardroom. He was a tall, slender man with a genteel manner and a calm and calming face. His crisp, perfectly ironed, bright-white full-length *dishdasha* added to the elegance of the rich wood interiors. He exuded Arabian graciousness and hospitality, greeting the three warmly and welcoming them into the room.

The room was a museum of Islamic art mixed with photographs of leaders throughout the Middle East, Europe, and the United States. The most striking were two large black-and-white photographs side by side, images of Dubai in 1960 and today. The eight board members stood up and were introduced to the team. They varied in age from their late twenties to close to eighty. The crisp white of their clothing was shining brightly in the room, adding to the grandeur of the place.

The chairman ordered special white Arabic coffee and water for everyone. Trays of exquisite dates and a variety of fruit were placed on the table.

The youngest board member shook Andy's hand and told him that he had his MBA from USC and owned a home in Belair. Andy had met him earlier when he was part of the selection committee touring the headquarters of the three finalists.

"Mr. Sykes, welcome to our country. I hope your visit here and your experience with us is to your satisfaction," the chairman said.

"Mr. Chairman, I love your country and have tremendous respect for what you, your citizens, and your leaders have accomplished. It is remarkable. I want to let you know that we have been treated graciously by everyone we have met. Thank you."

"Mr. Sykes, how much do you know about our history?"

"I have to admit my knowledge is limited to my two visits and what I have read in newspapers and periodicals," Andy replied sheepishly.

"I hope in your time here you will know about our history, our customs, our strengths, and our vulnerabilities. You are our guest of honor. Do not consider yourself an outsider or just a specialist we need. You are now part of our community. Anything you need, Elias and his team are available to support you," he continued.

"Mr. Chairman, your hospitality is overwhelming. As I shared with you earlier, I am humbled and honored to be part of your team. I pledge to you that you will get the best effort from me and my team to achieve your objectives," Andy responded.

"Thank you, Mr. Sykes. Before we discuss details of our project, I'd like for you to share with us your thoughts on the latest in AI applications for smart buildings and cities. I am fascinated by the impact of technology upon everything we do," the chairman said.

"I will be glad to. Let me begin by using Dubai's growth history as a model. Over the past fifty years, Dubai went through a remarkable transformation, from a small trading port city to an iconic metropolis," Andy said. "Nothing exemplifies the transformation better than its physical change, its buildings.

Your early buildings were the twenty-story variety, recycled to forty stories and recycled again to the tallest and most iconic.

"When you look at your new-built environment, your structures are designed and built in forms and shapes that were not possible too many years earlier. This ability to reinvent came about because of the explosive growth of technology, specifically the exponential growth of computing, algorithms driven by the application of artificial intelligence that allow designers and engineers to do things with our building that were unimaginable a few short years earlier. Today we have buildings that twist and turn and building skin with sensors that move to adjust to changes in the climate." Andy stopped for a sip of water.

"The designer using AI can, with specific algorithms, transform a building into a safe, organic, healthy, and living community. We as designers have always dreamt of creating such buildings but could not. Our capacity to create was limited to the tools available to us. Today, we have the tools that can provide unlimited data, options, variables, and possibilities to us in minutes. All we need to do is ask the right questions.

"The explosion of our technological tools has opened the door to experimentation and development of new and sustainable building materials, lighter, stronger, and cheaper, and new ways of doing construction to build faster, such as 3D printing, robotics in construction, security through face recognition. Very simply, our options of what we can build have grown significantly. All of this has become possible because of our abilities to use artificial intelligence," Andy continued.

"The software, the brains of the system, is designed through algorithms that collect and analyze millions of pieces of data and adjusts and directs how the building functions safely, securely, and consistently.

"As architects, we are responsible to direct and manage this tool to achieve the objective of integrating human behavior with the built environment. We have to ensure a building is sustainable, secure, and economical. AI gives us those tools. Our mission is to also make sure the building is absolutely safe against malfunction and secure against sabotage, internal or external."

Andy took another sip of water and continued.

"Let me try to simplify the definition of artificial intelligence. Call it the theory of big data combined with immense computing power, as a friend of mine described it. You ask the computer to calculate infinite variations of data in minutes or seconds that would have taken us weeks or months to calculate. It will ultimately give the optimal solution. Our job is to design the program, the equations, the commands to do its job, and it will. The programming team of designers, engineers, and technology gurus has the task of designing the best program to achieve the objective, and we intend to do just that." This time, Andy took a sip of the white Arabic coffee, his first time.

"Mr. Sykes, this is fascinating," the chairman said. "Please tell me why, with all this technological capability, you still see what I feel are ugly and tortured buildings, at least in my opinion?"

"Excellent observation," Andy said, almost chuckling. "The fact is the technology, including AI, responds to what you direct it to do, the questions you ask, and the commands you provide. It is not the creator of good taste, creative design, or elegance. That is the job of the designer. Not all designers, unfortunately, have that talent, but many do."

"Fascinating. Thank you, Mr. Sykes. Now, how about cyber-security? We have a new element being introduced to our project, advanced hardware that we have been told will remove the current total reliance upon software," the chairman said.

"I will leave that for Bill Sorenson to address. This is the initiative that CTC will be leading. Bill, please go ahead," Andy said.

"Let me start by adding my appreciation on behalf of CTC to be part of the team. We are honored to have the opportunity to implement a new cybersecurity system we believe will be the most significant new development in the defense against cyberattack, for whatever reason. It has been our privilege to have been your cyber-security adviser over the years," Bill Sorenson said, as he sat up and straightened his tie.

"Research to develop such hardware has been ongoing for years, with some success. It was necessary to develop such hardware that creates a physical firewall, leaving the cyber attacker only one option, and that is physical destruction. The successes achieved were major breakthroughs. They were limited, however, to individual computers by the introduction of advanced processors.

"What we are planning for Al Bustan is hardware to protect an entire network. We have been successful for a limited number of individual computers. For Al Bustan, we are not only protecting an individual network but also a series of networks, which would be the standard for tall buildings and large facilities." Bill looked around the room and took a sip of water.

"That is fascinating, Mr. Sorenson. How will you do that?" Abdulla Amin, the young board member, said as he leaned over, moving his white head scarf over to one side.

"Here is where Mr. Sykes comes in, the master of technology in tall buildings. It involves the use of sensors and processors throughout the building that will be connected to our hardware, which is the central server for the building," Bill said, as he fidgeted in his chair.

"Have you two worked together on any project like this before?" the young board member asked.

"No, we have not. For that matter, what we are planning has not been done before," Bill answered. "To make sure that what we are proposing is indeed very successful, we plan to test it. We will use an existing building for the testing, a smaller building that will be provided to us by your company."

"If I may add," Elias interjected, "we already have the building identified. Our schedule is to start the testing process immediately, while the important work on Al Bustan proceeds as planned. There will be no loss of time or delays."

The chairman stood up, walked over to the cabinet, and pulled out two books. He gave one to Andy and one to Bill. "Mr. Sykes, Mr. Sorenson, please accept this book from us; it is about our history and our culture.

"I would like you to read it; that would honor me—not because I wrote it but because I want you to feel welcome in our country. On behalf of the board, we look forward to getting our project underway, a project that is our crown jewel."

Andy, Bill, and Ayman stood up and shook hands with all the board members. Then they left the board room, carrying their books written by the chairman about the UAE.

9

THE YOUNG MAN sat in a chair facing two men and an older woman. One of the men was an Emirati, at least he was dressed like one. He appeared to be in charge. He was tall and large, an intimidating presence. He stared at the young man for a few minutes before he spoke.

"Ali, are you clear about the plan?" he asked.

"Yes, sir, I am," the young man, named Ali, replied. He sat up and straightened his red tie in a slightly oversized gray suit. He was careful to avoid looking directly at the big man.

"No radio or cell phones are to be used except for the one I gave you. That goes for the entire team. Is that clear?" the large man asked.

"Yes, sir. We already instituted total silence."

"Your only communication is with Selma through the agreed-upon channel. Under no circumstances are you to contact her any other way. Is that clear? The only time you contact us is through the coded messages we gave you," the leader said, as he placed his large hands on the old wooden table.

"Yes, sir. Very clear," Ali replied.

"Alright. You can go now. Good luck, Ali."

"Thank you, sir." The young man got up and left.

"Selma, is everything in place?" the leader asked the woman.

"Yes, sir. We are ready. The room is secure, with the necessary arrangements as you ordered." She started coughing.

The big man stared at her, and she immediately stopped coughing.

"Just a slight cold, sir. But there is one thing we need to be aware of," she said.

"What is that?"

"There are men watching the architect. They try to appear not so obvious, but we spotted them quickly. I think they were looking for who may be following the architects. They never spotted us," Selma explained.

"They are security. Make sure they don't see you," the leader said.

"The Americans have convinced the people at Pinnacle Enterprises that they are simply architects here to design a building for them. Total nonsense. Our suspicion has been confirmed. They are not good people." He spoke with authority and determination. "We cannot allow them to continue. We have to accelerate our timetable. In fact, this whole show is a charade."

He stopped. The other two looked at him, waiting for his direction.

"Our challenge is we don't know where they are hiding the package, a package that we believe is a large box that contains not only drugs but also some form of a new weapon. Our friend is trying to find out. We don't know where or what. Our orders are to continue the search for the box and destroy it, or we stop its delivery. The only way we can stop the delivery is to stop the people who are involved. I am sure in time they will bring other people. This will give us more time to develop countermeasures, but the first step is to find the box," the leader of the group said.

Selma was quiet, and so was the other man. She stood up, nodded, and left the room.

The building was an old apartment complex in Sharjah, UAE, next to Dubai. Selma was walking slowly, almost limping. The air was dusty, and she covered her mouth with the white hijab she was wearing as she started coughing uncontrollably. She walked to the bus that would take her to her apartment.

10

MARY WAS PACKING her paperwork and everything else she needed from her office for the trip to Dubai, when her phone rang. It was Tim Patterson, the deputy director. Mary mumbled something under her breath and picked up. "Hi, Tim. I am getting ready to head out to the airport. What's up?"

"Good luck in Dubai. Just a reminder: I want regular reports. Like I said, a lot of people are watching this," Tim said.

"Yes, Tim, I know. You have been very emphatic about this. I will report back often," Mary replied.

"I have to report to the director daily on this—his orders. You understand that he cannot hear about this project from anyone but me. You have to make sure that if you have any information, you call me immediately. You got that?"

"This is the tenth and last time I will tell you this: Yes, I get it. Yes, you will be the first person I call about any new information I get. Goodbye," Mary said, fuming as she hung up.

Mary took the elevator to the garage, found her Toyota SUV, and headed toward Reagan Airport. She had insisted on driving her car and would only request an agency car and driver if needed.

Natalie and Rusty were waiting for her, each with their backpack. Mary had parked her car in the designated area and was walking toward the two, carrying her brown leather bag.

"Rusty, you have what we need?" Mary asked.

"Yes, I have. I have already coordinated with our team in Dubai. They are set," Rusty answered.

"Mary, any idea how long we will be in Dubai?" Natalie asked.

"Don't know. We will have some idea once we know what is going on," Mary answered.

"Okay, here we go," Natalie said as they climbed the stairs to the agency plane.

Once en route, Mary took out a folder and started to read it for the second time. She looked up; Natalie and Rusty were waiting to hear what she discovered.

"I received a handwritten note from General Pitman. Bottom line, this hardware is real; security people like it and hope it can be the answer to beef up cybersecurity. That is all good. Here is the hitch: it is CTC. The company is highly respected and has worked on numerous sensitive assignments for the Pentagon. Here is where it gets interesting. This particular project in Dubai has raised eyebrows. Why test this equipment in Dubai, in a commercial building, no matter how close of an ally the UAE is? There are murmurs of commercial interests maybe driving this, which is fine; CTC is a private company. But remember that the CIA is also supportive of this project. Well, we will find out. Natalie, did you find out anything more about how this hardware works?" Mary asked.

"Pretty much what you have discovered, with one exception. According to our own CIA researchers, the proposed CTC hardware is more advanced than anything they have seen or proposed. There are rumors that the machine, with the right modifications, can become a lethal cyber weapon, not sure what or how. There is no hard evidence to substantiate the assumption; it is what a highly skilled technical expert in the agency believes. That's one theory why all this assumption and buzz," Natalie said.

"Interesting. Keep digging," Mary said, as she reclined her seat and closed her eyes.

11

ANDY WAS AT the airport waiting for Jennifer and Bob to arrive (they were on the same Emirates Airlines flight from LAX), when his cell phone buzzed. It was Bill. He wanted to meet the next day to clear up any misunderstandings and start working on the plan. Andy agreed to ten in the morning and said that Bob Thornton, his boss, would be joining them.

He spotted the two coming out. He waved and held both arms out for Jennifer, who ran toward him. They embraced, followed by a long, passionate kiss, ignoring Bob, who stood there smiling and delighted to see Andy. Jennifer had on soft gray pants, a white blouse, and tennis shoes. She held Andy's hand as they started walking to the exit.

Andy had a car and driver waiting, and they all stepped in: Bob in front, and Jennifer and Andy in the back, locked in an embrace. She started looking at the scenery like a mesmerized schoolgirl. Andy couldn't stop smiling. The weather was perfect for early November.

Jennifer had seen pictures of Dubai with its iconic buildings, but to see it in person was a whole different experience. "Everything is so modern, so contemporary," she told Andy. "Is any of the traditional Islamic architecture preserved?"

They arrived at the hotel; Bob checked in, and Jennifer and Andy went to the junior suite, which was exquisite. A basket of fruit and dates sat in the middle of the table. She put her arm around Andy and told him how much she loved him. Just then, the bellman brought in Jennifer's suitcase and proceeded to explain everything about the suite and how wonderful the room was. *That deserved a good tip,* Andy thought as he left the room.

Jennifer proceeded to take off Andy's clothes. He very gently grabbed her hand, and they went to the living room, where a bottle of Moët & Chandon was in a bucket of ice, waiting. Jennifer screamed with joy. It was her favorite champagne. He poured the champagne, grabbed Jennifer's hand, and walked back to the bedroom. They did not finish drinking, when Andy began to take her clothes off. His were already gone. They were naked in bed, full of love and passion. The sexual energy was powerful, passionate, and gentle.

At 8:00 p.m., Andy showered and got dressed for the evening. He told Jennifer he would be downstairs for a cocktail in the lobby with Bob to bring him up to date. She could join them before nine, when Ayman and his wife would be joining them for dinner. Andy left the room and headed downstairs.

Bob was waiting for him at the bar on the ground floor. He looked fresh and relaxed. Andy ordered a Belvedere vodka martini; Bob was drinking red wine. They raised their glasses, a salute to their success.

Bob told Andy about Tyler joining the firm and the eagerness he expressed to be in Dubai with them. Andy said, "That would be a great idea as things are moving faster than I had anticipated."

It was quiet at the bar. Only one other customer, at the other end, was talking to someone on his cell phone. Seated away from the bar was Ali, reading the *Al Khaleej Times.* The bartender brought two bowls of pistachios and spicy almonds. Andy took one of the almonds, inspected it, and then placed it in his mouth.

"Try one of these, Bob; they are good," Andy said before briefing him about his meeting at the company headquarters with the

CEO, his top two lieutenants, the chairman, and the board. He also told Bob that Bill Sorenson, the senior VP of CTC, was there.

"Andy, sounds like it all went well. Did you go into details regarding the contract, fees, and scope? Their expectations?" Bob asked.

"Not the details. It looks like they have accepted what we have proposed; in fact, they gave us verbal authorization to proceed and will send it to us in writing. It doesn't appear there will be any problems having the contract signed this week." Andy picked up his martini glass and took a sip. He licked his lips in obvious satisfaction.

"Good work, Andy. How about the cybersecurity issue? Remember, we had concerns about the Boston company and how we deal with them," Bob said.

The bar and lobby were beginning to get lively and noisy with people laughing, chatting, and celebrating. There was a mix of nationalities, young and old. Andy turned around and took a sweeping look at the growing crowd. He peeled a couple of large pistachios, imported from Iran, and placed them one by one in his mouth.

"You recall that the project, as we initially proposed, was primarily focused on the use of technology and AI as we have done historically but taken to a higher level by introducing new hardware for the security. That focus is still there but has shifted slightly, giving greater weight to cybersecurity by adding a testing of the hardware to start, separate from the main project," Andy said. "The project has almost become two projects. One is the master planning of Al Bustan that includes design of the overall development and tower; the other emphasis is on cybersecurity, which, at least for now, appears to be a high priority."

Bob was sipping his red wine after munching on a couple of spicy almonds.

"The cybersecurity plan, as we were told, has been blessed by our two governments. CTC claims they have our Department of

Defense's approval for the placement of this hardware in a commercial building," Andy added. "What's new is the emphasis on testing the hardware, which they have proposed. Now it seems that the testing will be done on an existing facility, a new wrinkle that we were not aware of. I am not sure if this is something to be concerned about."

"Wait a minute, Andy. A plan like this, which involves two governments and highly classified technology, does not just happen at the last minute. This must have been known and planned before they solicited the request for proposals and before they interviewed us."

"I agree. You are right. If you recall, when I had lunch back in LA with the executive of Cyber Technologies, and you couldn't join us, he made reference to it. I dismissed it as simply part of the process. He didn't give us much detail," Andy replied.

"Andy, did you know about this before you got here?" Bob asked.

"Before the interview, no, I did not. In general terms, I assume I should have known. There were red flags. I didn't ask too many questions," Andy said.

"We need to have all the facts, Andy—exactly what this might mean to us," Bob said.

"If you recall, we received the Request for Proposals, directly from the client, Pinnacle Enterprises. We were surprised but also delighted. That same week, we received a call from a senior executive from CTC. They told us they do quite a bit of cybersecurity work in the UAE for private companies, including Pinnacle. They had worked with Pinnacle and recommended to them that we be sent the RFP. They claimed they knew of our reputation.

"In other words, they were responsible for us being included to receive the request for proposals in the first place," Andy said. "We included them on our team, and they were given the lead role as the experts in the field. We had checked them out and found out that our newly appointed national security adviser was the former CEO of the firm."

"I remember," Bob said.

"The day after we received the notice that we were selected and before I left for Dubai, I received a call from the same executive of the company. He told me he was in LA and needed to meet with us, urgently and confidentially, he claimed. We met for lunch. You couldn't make it. That's when he told me about the other initiative, testing the hardware on an existing building. The purpose was to make sure the security plan works." Andy said.

"Why didn't you tell me? You realize this may be a significant change," Bob said.

"Bob, trust me, I wanted to. I simply did not think it was that big a deal. He insisted this was routine, but it was important to be kept secret. That's the nature of this kind of work, he stated. He was persuasive. He kept reminding me that our assignment just grew, and so would our fees. There would be no haggling on fees. He also reminded me of the involvement and support of the two governments," Andy said.

"For God's sake, Andy, how the hell do you expect to keep something like this secret? What will you tell your team? How do you hide the work in the contract?"

"Bob, there is no need for secrecy or hiding the testing in the contract. I am terribly sorry about this. I wish I had told you, but I didn't. I didn't think it was a big deal. It is also a great opportunity. Cutting-edge technology. It will immediately take us to the level we always dreamed of. Not to mention the fees. Besides, it may turn out to be nothing. I mean, nothing to worry about."

"You may be right. You know how I am; I don't like surprises," Bob said as he took another sip of his wine.

"Bill Sorenson, the CTC executive in charge of the project, will be here tomorrow morning to give us details about the plan, the hardware, and how we expect to manage the process," Andy said, as he watched Jennifer approaching them. She was in a blue dress with a white shawl around her shoulders. Her hair was twisted up in a curl, and she had two large silver loop earrings. She looked radiant.

"Hi, guys, did you solve the world's problems?" she said as Andy ordered a Manhattan for her, as per her specifications for her favorite cocktail.

"We only solved the problems in the Western Hemisphere," Bob said as he gave her a hug.

Before they could finish their drinks, Ayman and his wife, Hania, showed up to welcome Jennifer and join them for dinner. Hania was tall, thin, and elegant. She looked striking with her dark hair and soft-white dress. Jennifer felt an immediate connection with her.

"I hope you don't mind, but I took the liberty to reserve a table for us in one the best Italian restaurants in Dubai," Ayman said.

"The restaurant is on the gulf, where you will experience the gulf breeze. The food is exquisite, and their wine selection is the best," he said.

The three nodded in excitement, and Jennifer said, "I'm ready. Let's go."

As they left the hotel, they didn't pay attention to the young man sitting by a table next to an older woman who was wearing a white hijab. They were chatting amiably and drinking tea, with some pastries on the table.

As the party of three Americans and two new guests left the hotel, the young man picked up his cell phone, texted a message, and put the phone away. The message simply said, "Three and two." They finished their tea, paid the bill, and left the hotel.

12

HANIA CAME BY around ten the next morning to take Jennifer on a tour of the city. Jennifer suggested they have coffee at the hotel before they leave. Hania said no; she had a special place in mind.

In the car, Hania was the guide, pointing out the major attractions. Traffic jams, cranes, and new buildings were everywhere. The hustle and the noise of cars and of people did not seem to disturb Jennifer. She peppered Hania with questions, and Hania seemed to genuinely enjoy Jennifer's curiosity. She would often grab Jennifer's arm and point to a building or some iconic structure, her dark hair following her pointing hand.

She told Jennifer they would start with the most iconic attraction, the Burj Khalifa, the tallest human made structure in the world, located near the largest mall in the world, the Dubai Mall, with over one thousand shops. As they approached the tower, designed by Skidmore Owens and Merrill (SOM) of Chicago, Jennifer was twisting and turning in her seat, in awe of the 2,722-foot-tall tubular-shaped towers with 163 occupied stories and containing the first Armani hotel.

Hania parked in the massive parking garage for the twelve-million-square-foot Dubai Mall and took the elevator inside. Jennifer thought it would take a month just to walk to all the shops.

"Well, Jennifer, what do you think?" Hania said, holding Jennifer's hand in the elevator.

"We are both married to architects; we live with their passions and appreciate great buildings. All I can say is wow; this is truly awesome. How can this be? How can they do it, built so well and so fast? How can they afford it?" Jennifer said.

The shops and restaurants were everywhere, with names like Armani, Prada, and Gucci. Hania found her favorite coffee shop, and they walked in. There were great seats for watching people, and they ordered coffee and pastries.

"Jennifer, I wanted to show you the mall first to appreciate the size and scale of this development. We will go outside to see the impressive Dubai fountains water feature and then go to Burj Khalifa. I have tickets for the express elevator to the one hundred and forty-eighth observatory floor. I think it is the one hundred and forty-eighth," Hania said.

"I am your follower, Hania, two steps behind you."

"I promise I won't lose you," Hania laughed. "Maybe later today we can go skiing?"

"I always wanted to ski indoors." They both laughed.

Shoppers were moving as shoppers do in New York and Paris— walking, talking, laughing, and pointing. They were diverse: Europeans of all kinds in elegant dresses or in shorts and jeans, Asians, Arabs. So many different nationalities.

"The children, the adults, the grandparents—everyone seems so relaxed and happy," Jennifer said.

"That is very true about the UAE. The mix of nationalities is amazing," Hania added.

"I wonder how they keep it all together. I am talking about orderly. You get the sense of it being fast-paced yet calm," Jennifer said.

As they were finishing their coffee, Jennifer asked Hania about her observation of the large Indian population.

"The Indian presence in the UAE goes back centuries, driven by closeness and trade. Some of the wealthiest families in Dubai are Indian or of Indian origin. The same goes for the many thriving companies. Well, it is time to go and observe the city from the sky." Hania stood up and grabbed Jennifer by the hand, and they started walking toward Burj Khalifa.

It took the express elevator less than a minute to get to the observation deck. They looked at the city below; it appeared so small from the sky. Jennifer was loving it, totally immersed in the enormity of the tower, when Hania gently touched her arm. "Jennifer, do you see that young man with the older woman walking around the perimeter?" she asked.

"Yes, I do. What about them?" Jennifer replied.

"I think they have been following us. I recognize them from the hotel lobby." Hania was alarmed.

Jennifer tried to look without being too obvious. "You're right, but it is probably a coincidence."

"Maybe. Maybe I am being paranoid, but I'm not a believer in coincidences," Hania said.

"Why would anyone want to follow us?"

"Two beautiful women. Why wouldn't they?" They both laughed an uneasy laugh.

Back in the car, Hania told Jennifer they were going to the historic part of Dubai near the old souks. They would have an authentic, traditional Arabic lunch, gulf style.

Jennifer had never seen so many shops that sold nothing but gold. It was overwhelming. Shoppers were everywhere. Hania asked if she wanted to buy a gift. Jennifer said she wanted to come back another day for shopping. She was hungry and couldn't wait to taste the local cuisine.

The restaurant was a fresh fish market on the water's edge. Fishermen brought their fresh variety from the gulf, rich with sea life. Hania and Jennifer selected their fish, both for starters and the main course, cooked in their choice of preparation and spicing. The fresh, warm Arabic bread came accompanied by a variety of vegetables and rice. It was a feast. Jennifer was in heaven.

"When people ask me what my favorite food is, my answer always is good food. This is beyond good food," Jennifer said.

On the way back to the hotel, Jennifer felt a strong kinship with Hania, as if she had known her a long time. Hania told Jennifer she and Ayman would like to invite her, Andy, and Bob to have brunch at their home. They would invite a few of their close friends. "The best day would be on the weekend," Hania said.

"That would be wonderful," Jennifer said.

13

THE CIA PLANE landed in Dubai with the three passengers: Mary, Natalie, and Rusty. Major Charles (Chuck) Garfield and a white Toyota SUV, the most common in the UAE, were waiting for them. They stepped in with their carry-ons and headed to the American consulate. The car was dispatched to them from the embassy in Abu Dhabi, 130 kilometers away.

"Major, it has been a while since London. Good to see you again. Let me introduce you to Rusty, our cyber guru, and Natalie, who you met in London," Mary said, once they were inside and the SUV was headed to the consulate.

"Good to see you, Mary and Natalie; that was a great effort in London, taking down the Hungarian cell. Nice to meet you, Rusty. So, Mary, what's the plan? I am surprised you are here, by the way. I know how busy you are with all the cyberattacks," the major said.

"Well, Major, we don't want to be here any longer than we have to be. This may be a wild goose chase; we plan to find out quickly. Natalie and Rusty will be staying at the safe house; two of our agents are waiting to debrief them. You and I will go over what you know, the lay of the land, and the next steps. I am meeting General Masoud this evening; hopefully he has more to tell us."

"Okay," the major agreed.

"Let's plan to meet again tonight after my meeting with the

general at the consulate, compare notes, and discuss the next steps. We'll have dinner at the consulate.

"Here's what I want to know: if this out-of-the-blue chatter about a potential terrorist attack is real, what this project is, who the players are, their backgrounds with the companies involved, what this hardware is, why the Department of Defense granted CTC a license for the commercial use of classified hardware, and anything else we can uncover. We need to find out the identity of the man found shot with a picture of the American architect in his pocket. That worries me. I'm hoping we wrap this up in a day or two and head back to Washington," Mary added.

The SUV arrived at the consulate, where Mary and the major were dropped off, and then proceeded to the safe house, where Natalie and Rusty would be staying. It was a villa in a large community, with four bedrooms, well decorated, and similar to many of the other villas, mostly being rented to expats.

———

"Okay, Major, what is going on? I don't get what all this noise is and why," Mary said, after she was settled and joined the major in one of the many secure conference rooms.

Before responding, the major got up and went to the table in the corner with a pot of coffee and a pitcher of ice water on it. He poured two cups of black coffee and brought them to the conference table, placing one in front of Mary.

"I had a fresh pot made. I knew how much you enjoy a cup of java like I do," he said.

"Thank you for remembering," Mary said, as she took a nice gulp of the fresh coffee. She stood up; she was wearing a light-gray pantsuit and a white blouse, and she looked fit. She stretched her arms and sat back in her chair. "I think I will hit the gym for half an hour before meeting the general. Always helps when traveling.

I learned that from you. But first, Chuck, back to business. What is going on here?"

"This whole thing is strange. I have met with the national security people and reviewed the materials from the airwaves and the chatter; it all appears to be a call for defense against us, the Americans. It claims that we are planning to install some kind of weapon, maybe a cyber weapon, in this project. It doesn't seem to say who the target of this weapon is supposed to be," the major said.

"Any idea who's behind this? Iranians, Russians, terrorist groups, who?" Mary asked.

"We don't know; we don't think it is terrorist groups or lone wolves. We have not been able to get to the source. That tells me these are a sophisticated bunch, which narrows it down to a state or state-sponsored group. Many countries may have the capability, with Russia and Iran on top of the list, especially Iran because it's only twenty miles away. The bigger question is why. Why would they do that because of a project like many others in Dubai that is just getting underway? It does not add up," he said.

"Any theories? Is this an effort to undermine the project? Maybe this is a commercial effort to sabotage rather than a national security concern?" Mary said.

"Well, Mary," Chuck started, as he got up. He walked over to the table, brought the coffee pot back, and refilled both cups. "Something is rotten in China. It does not make any sense, no matter how you look at this. The targeted weapon, while a type of advanced hardware, is not a weapon. The company is highly respected, and the team hired to do the work is from a well-known design firm. So where is the threat? The only potential wild card is CTC; they are a cybersecurity company well connected to US security and defense agencies."

"Interesting. Very interesting," Mary said.

14

BILL SORENSON ARRIVED at the hotel; Bob and Andy were in the lobby waiting for him. After introductions, they found a remote table and ordered Turkish coffee, which arrived with a few quarter-sized cookies and always with a glass of water. Bill took a sip of the coffee, looked around the room, and then picked up the spoon and started spinning it slowly on the table.

"I'm sorry, Bill, that I was not able to join you and Andy for lunch when you were in LA," Bob said, starting the discussion.

"I'm sorry I missed you too. We will do it again when I am back there. I must apologize for the way this started. I don't blame you for having concerns. I promise that was not our intention," Bill said.

"Let me get right to the point, Bill. This project, Al Bustan, is without a doubt a dream project for any architect. What is not clear is the application of technology in ways never done before," Bob said.

"We assembled a great team, some of the best specialists in their fields. We literally worked day and night putting together a proposal we are extremely proud of. We know we can create what our client wants. We were excited to get started; we were ready," Bob said, as he took a sip of water.

"Now we . . . I mean, I find out that this project is not quite what I assumed it to be. Now I find out there is another, separate project added to the Al Bustan project. A project that involves national security. A project that is supposed to be for the purpose of testing the system. What is troubling is the cloud of secrecy around it. We are asked to incorporate new hardware in the security system, but we don't even know what it is or how it works. You can imagine our concerns, not to mention those of the other team members when they come onboard. We are dedicated to teamwork and transparency."

Bob paused.

"Bill, we have way too many questions that need answers. I hope you can clear the air for us and address our concerns. We may be overreacting, maybe not. We need to hear all the facts and have our questions and concerns addressed."

"Bob, I understand. That's why I am here. Please, go ahead and ask me any questions you have. My mission is to make sure you and Andy are very comfortable. We need you," Bill said.

"Okay, Bill. To start with, why the secrecy? What is this hardware? You make it sound like a special high-security defense issue, which leaves us wondering if there is more to it."

Bill hesitated briefly and took a sip of water. "Let me first give you an overview of the circumstances that ultimately led to this project. Our company, CTC, has been at the forefront of cybersecurity; that is what we do. I believe we are the best in the field. To stay there, we are constantly working on research to develop better hardware and software to defend our government, businesses, financial institutions, infrastructure, defense systems, and others." Bill took a sip of coffee.

"A couple of years ago, one of the major facilities owned by Pinnacle was hacked; they managed to control the building functions, including the HVAC system, electrical, security, and telecommunications. The hackers were demanding ransom from Pinnacle. The UAE Ministry of Defense, for whom we are upgrading their cyber defenses and testing new hardware, brought us in to assist Pinnacle. We did. In a relatively short time, we managed to remove the ransomware from the facilities network without paying any ransom. That led to working with Pinnacle regarding their next major development project, Al Bustan. That is why we are here today." Bill stopped and took another sip of water.

"Bill, how does the background you outlined fit with what we are doing? The main issue we are to understand is this hardware. The server you are proposing, what is it? How does it work?" Andy asked.

"Andy, let me address the licensing first. The US and the UAE have strong national security ties; they are also targets of hackers' malware, spyware, and ransomware. Both governments work closely with their private sector, assisting them in their ongoing cybersecurity challenges. Our government is eager to test new technologies to be used by all users, public and private. Not only did they approve the license, but the Department of Defense is hoping for positive results to be applied universally." Bill finished his glass of water and put his spoon on the table.

"As you both may know," he continued, "our former CEO is the national security adviser in the current administration. He is a strong advocate of robust defensive strategies, but more importantly, he is a stronger advocate for going on the offensive. He is passionate in his belief our superior technical capabilities are superior to any of our adversaries, and he wants to keep it that way. To start with, he wants those defensive and offensive strategies implemented. He has mandated this as urgent and a high priority.

"The US government has also concluded that Iran is a threat. Considering the animosity between the two countries, their commitment to become a nuclear power, our crippling sanctions, and, most worrisome, Iran's influence and interference in the neighborhood, the gulf states, because of their proximity, are particularly vulnerable to their threats. They are also very cautious not to antagonize Iran," Bill continued.

"Thank you, Bill. Very helpful. Now back to the main questions: what is the hardware, how does it work, and how will it be implemented?" Bob asked.

"You both know that one of the most explosive growth areas in technology that has not received the attention it deserves is IoT, the Internet of Things, connecting object to object. The new miniature and powerful processors have opened the door wide for all kinds of applications from smart vehicles, lighting systems, security systems, safety, infrastructure, and on and on, impacting every aspect of our lives." Bill stood up for a quick stretch.

"Now," he continued, feeling energized, "what has made the IoT possible were technological advances, more powerful processors, wireless technology, and the explosion in AI. Why not apply it to a large facility, a building such as the one in Al Bustan?

"We have developed hardware that does that, an advanced server that acts as the brains of the building and is remotely connected to the sensors and processors, carefully placed throughout the building. This provides efficiency for the functions of the building and its security, both physical and cyber. That is where you come in—placing the sensors, connecting to, and programming the server. We have experimented with this technology and an AI-driven system on a smaller scale but not on a project of this magnitude. If we succeed, and we are confident we will, this would be a significant breakthrough."

"Very interesting, Bill. For us, it is a vision of a healthier, grander future. We create skins that move and adjust to climate conditions, buildings that respond safely to wind, storms, earthquakes. Organic buildings with organic farms. We use AI to analyze for us in minutes what might otherwise take months," Bob added.

"Exactly. That is exactly why we need you," Bill said. "Andy, correct me if I am wrong. You place censors throughout the building, especially the building skin. They are connected to the server, the center, the brain. You design the programs, the instructions, and the commands that order how the building acts. You have programmed thousands, tens of thousands of variables and conditions. Your use of AI allows us to do that and more. You even wrote a paper on the subject for the international conference for tall buildings last year. Now, what we are asking of you is to take those capabilities to a much higher level. We want you to use AI capabilities and program the building to deter any cyberattack. In other words, your computer systems inside the building are safe," Bill said.

"Wait a minute . . . cyber defense is a programmable defense, not the physical building. That is a whole new parameter. A command to the computer is not physical. It is ether, waves that you can't see." Andy was puzzled.

"Okay, Andy. What if we gave you the ability to see what is coming? Could you have the building programmed to defend against it?" Bill asked. "Think of it this way," he continued. "Think of it as a firewall; we place firewalls in our computer for security against hackers. We place firewalls around a small network. Why not a firewall around a building? We have been limited by the sheer size of the effort. The game has changed; we have almost unlimited data collection and calculating power through AI. By connecting the interior of the building to the exterior skin, it allows us to literally program the building," Bill said.

"The two questions that immediately come to mind are, do we have the data and computing power that allows us to accomplish this? Second, let's say we do have the capabilities and can accomplish this; why the secrecy? The effort can simply be part of the Al Bustan project without getting involved in national security," Bob said.

"Yes, we do have those capabilities with the new hardware," Bill replied.

"I am sure you must know the enormity of what you are suggesting," Andy said. "The sheer volume of information in all forms legitimately coming into the building. Millions or billions of data per minute is not out of the ordinary. We need enormous server capacity to do this. I can't imagine how and where we can get this capability. Secondly and most importantly, how do you differentiate the good waves from the bad, and, finally, how do you turn it around. Sonar? Radar? A new secret weapon?" Andy took a deep breath, waiting for answers.

"Robert, Andy, we believe we have those capabilities. They have not been tested on this scale. That is where you guys come in. We want you to work with us. You with special skills regarding technology-driven buildings and our side with technology, fast computing capacity, and the latest in AI research. We believe we can do it. Al Bustan moves forward as planned, while we work together on the other part. If it does not meet our requirements, Al Bustan is not delayed." Bill stopped and picked up the spoon, slowly moving it around the table.

"This is a lot to absorb, Bill. For starters, we need to know what you know. We need to understand that what we are dealing with is cybersecurity. We need to examine the server, to learn how it works and how it is programmed, before we start any of the work. Remember, Bill, I am the project manager, responsible for all aspects of the project," Andy said.

Bill tried to respond but hesitated. He stood up again for another stretch, spotted the waiter, motioned for him to come over, and ordered another espresso and more water. Bob and Andy also ordered the same.

"Well, that may be a bit of a problem, more a timing issue. You need to have security clearance to allow you access. It is not high security, but it will take time," Bill said.

"Wait a minute, Bill. I have to have access to and become totally familiar with the hardware before we start anything. That is not an option," Andy demanded.

"Do you have anyone on your team who has security clearance?" Bill asked.

"No, we don't. Even if we had, I am in charge of and responsible for the project. I will not move ahead with the testing unless and until I understand what the proposed security system is. I will inform Pinnacle; they are expecting us to start ASAP," Andy replied.

"Didn't you just hire an architect with security clearance?" Bill asked.

"Yes, we did. Tyler Grant. He is arriving tonight," Bob replied.

"That may help, but it will not solve the problem. I have to have access. Secondly, I assume that by the terms of security clearance, he may not be able to share it anyway. Bill, I have no choice but to let Pinnacle know," Andy stated.

"Okay," Bill replied after a long pause, twirling the spoon faster. "I will contact the defense department and also my boss to see what they can do on their end to expedite the clearance. In the meantime, please wait until I get back to you before you talk to Pinnacle." Bill stood up, shook their hands, and left.

———

The young man several tables away had been sitting there the whole time, sipping on Turkish coffee, reading the local newspaper, and expertly taking pictures of the three Americans. When the heavyset American with the large belly left the hotel, he sent a message on his cell phone: coded numbers.

———

Andy looked at Bob and started scratching his head, a habit since he was young.

"This is a strange twist. It is clear to me CTC does not want our control or, for that matter, our knowing too much about this server. I think we should hold our ground; we do not start the server-testing portion until I have access to the equipment."

"I agree. If we don't now, it will be difficult, if not impossible, later. I also recommend that we give Bill twenty-four hours to come up with a solution before you call Pinnacle. Tyler is arriving later tonight; he wanted to get together for a quick review before we call it a night. Are we going to dinner at Ayman's home?"

"Yes, he is picking us up at seven. I am going to the room and see what Jennifer is up to. See you later, Bob."

Andy went back to his room. Jennifer was at the desk watching CNN while working on emails. Andy leaned over and gave her a kiss. "Hi, sweetheart. How did your meeting go?" she asked.

"Well. Interesting. Intriguing," Andy replied.

"Is the project real?" Jennifer asked.

"The project is great. The security issue is unnerving."

15

THE OLDER MAN stood up from behind his desk and grabbed his cane to lean on as he walked around his desk to the sitting area, where another man was sitting. He also stood up when Ayman walked in.

"Hello, Ayman, good to see you," the older man said. "I want you to meet General Masoud, director of security."

"Of course. It is an honor to meet you, Sheikh Masoud," Ayman said.

"My pleasure, Ayman. I have heard many good things about you. I want to thank you for your loyalty and for assisting us," the general said.

Ayman was well aware that he was in the company of two of the most influential individuals in the UAE. They both exuded authority and had a strong presence.

They sat down, and the older gentleman ordered tea.

"Ayman, it appears the Americans are pushing hard to get this project underway," the general said.

"We also know they are having some difficulty getting the pieces together to allow them to move forward. It appears that most of the team is here: the design team, the Cyber Technologies group, the CIA operatives. Let me share with you some security concerns. What is frustrating is that every lead we pick up about the source of the chatter has been a dead end. We have picked up a number of people who were on our list, but they told us nothing. Nobody seems to know anything. My conclusion is we are dealing with a sophisticated group. Could be one person, but most likely it is a team."

"What have you found out?" the old man asked.

"Nothing more than what you already know. The team is here to start the work," Ayman said. "What I am puzzled about," he added, "is this new hardware that we, the design team, know nothing about. I will have a much better idea once we know."

"Any idea when that would be? Remember, Ayman, we are supportive of the new security system; we are hoping it works. This potential threat bothers me if there is some validity to these concerns," the general said.

"I wish I knew. Right now, I don't see anything to be concerned about," Ayman said.

"We are quite concerned about these potential threats. I recommend you stay close to the American architect. Find out what he knows and what his concerns are," the old man said.

"I will." Ayman rose and shook hands. "By the way," he said as he started to leave, "my wife and the architect's wife felt there were people following them, specifically following the architect's wife. Any thoughts who that may be?"

The two men looked at each other but didn't say anything.

"I will have some of our people there to follow them for protection. Don't tell the architects. I don't want to alarm them," the general said.

"Thank you," Ayman said and left.

"What do you think?" the old man asked. "Iranians?"

"Could be," the general replied. "But I am not sure."

"Mary Tobias, my old friend with the CIA, is in Dubai. We are meeting again this afternoon," General Masoud said.

"We need to get to the bottom of this. We cannot get entangled with some terrorist group. What worries me most is that this plan would inflame Iran, which is only twenty miles away from us." The older man was clearly concerned. He was a man of few words, but his words counted.

16

BILL SORENSON WAS not pleased. He was worried. His staff was in the dark. Any delays to finalize the installation of the complete system could place it in jeopardy. Too many people were asking questions, demanding answers. If this project unraveled, many heads would roll, including his.

He was well aware of the fact that he may become the fall guy. The sacrificial lamb. Including jail time. He had to protect himself.

He picked up the phone and dialed the private number of the senior VP of CTC. Jeff Milbank picked up immediately. "Hi, Bill, what's wrong?" he said.

"Jeff, we need to meet. I can be in New York by tomorrow afternoon; we can meet in the evening at the Four Seasons. It is essential our partner is there too."

Jeff Milbank hesitated. He knew this had to be very urgent for Bill to request a meeting. He could not ignore it. Including Sam Kopitski from the Sebastian Corporation was highly unusual. Something must have gone wrong. "Okay, Bill, I will be there. I'll call Sam to join us. We'll meet you at six in your suite. First, give me some idea what this is all about."

"I will when we meet," Bill said.

"Bill, don't hang up. Be careful; stay the course. Please don't try anything crazy," Jeff pleaded.

"Don't worry; I won't. See you in New York tomorrow night," Bill said and hung up.

He dialed another number, and Elias Khoury picked up. "Hi, Bill, what's going on? Everything alright?"

"We may have a problem. Andy Sykes does not have security clearance to have access to the server. He is stating that he will not work on the security without access to the server," Bill said.

"You told me he doesn't need it. What's going on?" Elias said.

"We are not ready to share access yet. I need time. I will be in New York tomorrow and back the next day. I will iron it out," Bill said.

"You'd better figure it out and fast. I told you we cannot lose any time. I have already authorized the team to start work on the buildings; that will not be slowed down. Figure it out, and see me as soon as you get back," Elias said.

"Elias, wait. I have to be careful who I share this information with. I can't risk the possibility of this hardware falling into the wrong hands, not now, not until we have it tested and ready."

"You should have anticipated all this ahead of time," Elias said.

"Tomorrow I will meet with the architects. I will not take the box with me. I will explain how the box works and share with them the codes to activate it. I will tell them we are fast tracking the clearances for them. I need those few days," Bill said.

"I don't like it, but do what you must," Elias said and hung up.

17

BILL SORENSON WAS in his suite at the New York Four Seasons. He was pacing, deep in thought, worried about his exposure. If this plan failed and he was exposed, he would definitely land in jail. If he went to jail, he would be damned if he went in alone.

There was a knock on the door. He went and opened it. His boss, Jeff Milbank, and Sam Kopitski, the senior VP of Sebastian Corporation, walked in. After greetings, they went to the living room and sat down. He offered them drinks, and both requested scotch on the rocks. He made one for himself as well, his second.

"Thank you both for coming on such short notice," Bill said.

"Of course. We had to come; you sounded as if the sky was falling," Jeff said. They all laughed nervously.

"Maybe a little, right, Bill?" Sam added.

"Okay, seriously, Bill, what is going on that is so urgent?" Jeff asked.

"I am very concerned about our plans being exposed and possibly compromised. Our partner's team members are asking a lot of questions and demanding answers. The internal security in the UAE, we hear, is getting involved. A team from the CIA has arrived in Dubai, asking questions. Most disturbing are the rumors that Iranians or some other group is involved. They obviously have heard about our project," Bill said, clearly agitated.

"Remember, Bill, we talked about this early on. We expected some of this," Sam said.

"That is correct; we did talk about this and the best way to handle it. What do you suggest we do, Bill? It is too late to change course. We have other partners. We made promises," Jeff added.

"I warned you from the beginning that tying the two together was unnecessary and added risk. To get down to the bottom of this, if things go south on us, I will be left exposed. Neither of you shows up anywhere. I cannot be the fall guy." Bill exhaled.

"Look, Bill, you are not going to be left high and dry. We are all in this together. The course we are on is the right course. Think about that. As far as any of the players know, we are elevating cyber-security measures to a very high level never implemented before," Jeff stepped in.

"To ensure the accuracy and effectiveness of what we are recommending, we intend to test the system. That is why we have selected an existing building for the testing while plans are underway for Al Bustan. We have been consistent with our message."

"The problem we have is that people are questioning what we are saying. Some don't believe us. Some suspect sinister motives. Somehow either the message itself or the messaging is not resonating," Bill said. "The believability issue, as challenging as it may be, is not what worries me the most. What keeps me awake at night is the plan itself. With all due respect to you, Sam, I am not exactly sure the modified hardware works. I am taking your word for it."

"Aren't you a bit late getting cold feet?" Sam was not happy. "A reminder, Bill: we have other partners in this deal. They are not going to stand for last-minute nerves."

"Listen, Sam, I have not lost my nerve. I am a pragmatist. I am also cautious. This plan has a lot of moving parts. We have the central server, the black box, which is already in Dubai in a secure location. We have identified the building that would house it. We have identified the three satellite locations where the radio signals will be received and orders implemented. Any one of those receivers plus the command center can be compromised," Bill said.

"Bill, we have been through this. So what if they are discovered? Simple answer, they are part of the testing. Period. No one can know what this is until it is activated, not even then . . . until it is used," Jeff said.

"Or until someone gets a hold of the black box and finds a way to figure it out. A tough task but doable in the right skilled hands," Bill said. "One more thing: I need protection, a guarantee that I will not be left hanging if we are discovered."

"Bill, we are all in this together. What kind of guarantee do you want? If you go down, we go down," Sam said.

"I want ten million dollars in an account of my choosing that my family can access," Bill replied.

"Wow, Bill. This is totally unexpected. You are getting a huge cut when we are done, not this. You are blackmailing us. This is unacceptable," Jeff jumped in.

"No, I am not blackmailing anyone, Jeff. I am simply protecting myself and my family. I am well aware of how much money you two will make if it all works out. Think of this as my cut . . . in advance."

Jeff wanted to say something. He was angry and started getting up, when Sam put his hand on his arm and brought Jeff back down to his seat.

"Bill. I get it. I understand you are out there on the front line doing the heavy lifting, dealing with the challenges. I totally get it. Jeff, I don't think Bill is out of line. Let's think about this; a couple of people need to agree. Bill, give us a couple of days. I am certain we can work something out," Sam added. "In the meantime, where do you have the box? It is well protected, I assume," Jeff said.

"Yes, it is. I am going back to Dubai tonight to meet with Pinnacle and the architects, who requested a short meeting to clear the air, they said," Bill stated, without telling them where the server was.

"What do you think? How should we handle him?" Jeff asked Sam when they were alone in the elevator.

"Do nothing until we find the black box," Sam said.

18

"**E**LIAS, I RECOMMEND we get started with the Al Bustan project without the security piece. Wait the few days for Bill to get us the clearance we need. In the meantime, Bill will get us whatever information he is allowed to give us and go from there," Andy said in the meeting with Pinnacle that he and Bob requested.

"We need to be clear that we will not start work on the security until we know what it is and how it works. Please remember that we are still unsure how a server, any server, can accomplish what is being proposed," Bob said.

"Bob, Andy, you are right. We will follow your recommendations. I have instructed my team, Joseph and Mounir, to get the contract prepared for signature. In the meantime, you have been given the authority to start the work. Regarding the security, we will wait to go ahead full speed once you have examined the hardware and the plans to use it. Bill, make sure you get the necessary clearance as fast as you can. Let me know if you need assistance from our national security," Elias said.

"I will, thank you. Andy, I will call you tomorrow to get us started. I will walk you through the codes needed to activate the server without having the server available," Bill added.

"Thank you, Elias, very helpful. Bill, do you have a security mechanism that disables the server, if you have to?" Bob asked, as he stood up, ready to leave.

"Good question, Bob. Yes we do. It is a self-destruct mechanism, if breached without the proper codes," Bill said.

The rest of the team got up; they shook hands with Elias and started leaving.

"Good to see you all. I will see you again very soon. Bill, please stay back for a few minutes. I need to review some details," Elias said.

———

They all left except for Bill.

"We have overcome the first hurdle. You better make sure there are no more surprises and that this cyber system is what you assured us it would be," Elias said.

"I assure you there won't be any more surprises," Bill said.

"Alright. Now I need to know where the server is," Elias said.

"In a safe place in Dubai." Bill was fidgeting, caught off guard.

"Where in Dubai?" Elias demanded. Bill didn't respond.

"Where, Bill? I have to know."

"I can't say," Bill finally said after a long pause.

"What the hell? What do you mean you can't say? Who are you hiding this from? Me?" Elias asked, angry.

"No, Elias, of course not, not you."

"Then who?" Elias shouted.

"My partners," Bill said, knowing he had no choice.

"This is insane. Now I have changed my mind. I am not asking where the server is; I am demanding. Not only demanding—I insist you show me where it is right now, and I will meet you there. I want to see it."

Bill knew he had no choice; he gave Elias the address and said he would meet him there. Then he got up and left.

Elias stayed seated, staring at the clouds through the large window for a few moments. Then he calmly stood up, took his car keys, and left. He did not ask for his driver.

19

THE INTERNAL SECURITY building, headquarters of General Masoud and his sprawling operations, was imposing. It was built five years earlier under the direction and command of the general. It was the nerve center of Dubai security and the police force. General Masoud was waiting in his office when his aid escorted Mary and Major Garfield in.

The general stood up; his tall stature cut an imposing figure. It was well-known that underneath the outward friendly and gracious demeanor was a determined and demanding personality. He was dressed in his security uniform when he warmly greeted his two guests.

"Mary, welcome, welcome. Major, good to see you again," the general said with his perfect British accent, which he picked up in the years he spent in England, studying at Amherst.

"Great to see you, General; you look well," Mary said.

"Masoud, Mary. Call me Masoud, no formalities between us."

"Alright, Masoud. Your new facilities are impressive. I hope you can give us a quick tour," Mary said.

"Absolutely, Mary, let us go now. I will show you our war room; that is what we call our nerve center, our eyes and ears. We will discuss how we are monitoring potential terrorist attacks, criminal activity, or other potential threats to our security. It will show you how we are tracking Al Bustan."

The general led his guests to a large double door with a guard on each side. The guards saluted as they opened the doors. They entered a vestibule; there was a desk and a chair on the left wall, with a guard sitting. The guard stood up and saluted the general.

They opened the second door and entered the war room, an enormous space of electronic high-tech equipment. The concave wall was completely covered with large screens; each included at least twenty smaller screens. Each screen covered a segment of the city with a team of ten specialists manning each of the larger ones. Behind the specialists were two long curved tables, matching the screens; seated along the length of the tables were another group of specialists monitoring computer screens in front of them, with earphones on for listening and coordinating. The floor was three levels, allowing all parties a clear view of the screens.

"When I was given the position to be head of security, it was our mission to make Dubai a safer and more secure city than anywhere in the world. We trained over seventeen thousand police officers in our special academy. The training covered law enforcement, social interaction, assistance, and how to help our citizens, our expats, and our tourists. We installed kiosks throughout the city that were easily accessible to anyone in need of help so they could call us. We have installed cameras throughout our major public facilities, major buildings, parks, malls, streets, transit and bus stations, the airports, you name it. Our goal is to have cameras in all commercial buildings. Very simply, we want a secure and safe city without intrusion into our people's privacy.

"This facility is the center where the monitoring takes place. Notice the large screens: each represents a district or a special facility; the smaller screens are subareas. We can zero in where we need to probe further for greater detail if need be. The two rows behind the screens are specialists who also monitor cyber chatter; they are connected to another group in the adjacent facility specialized in cybersecurity. We have an integrated security system." The general described this to his guests with obvious pride and confidence.

"General, congratulations. This is the most impressive operation I have seen," Major Garfield said.

"Impressive, indeed. Congratulations, Masoud," Mary added.

"Thank you. Let's go back to my office and review Al Bustan," he said.

"Let me share with you what we know," the general said, back at his office. "The chatter on the airwaves is getting louder and darker. The message is consistent: what is being planned for Al Bustan is designed to harm. Who is being harmed or why is unknown; it simply repeats the message of a dangerous weapon by the Americans. Normally, this kind of cyber chatter we can trace relatively quickly. In this case, we have not been able to accomplish that, but we will in time. Whoever is behind this is sophisticated in cyber technology to get away with it as they have."

"Does that mean this is state-sponsored?" Mary asked.

"Seems that way or at least a very sophisticated group," he replied.

"Okay, that leads me to the next question: why the chatter all of a sudden? Why do they suspect this new hardware? Masoud, you have worked with our Department of Defense and the company CTC promoting the hardware; is there anything in your evaluations that makes you suspicious?" she asked.

"No, I don't see anything, and that is the problem. I am hoping it works on this large scale. More puzzling is this sudden chatter from nowhere," the general said.

"Our team believes this chatter may be deliberately planned, maybe to cause confusion, maybe to harm the project or divert the attention to something else," Major Garfield said.

"Actually, Major, we are beginning to think the same ourselves. One thing is troubling, however. The architect is being followed, we think. We have spotted a young man in the hotel lobby where the architects are staying, and he appears to be following them. We have not interfered yet, waiting to see if it leads to others. If true, this adds a different twist beyond online chatter. It is physical and real," the general said.

"You are absolutely right; this changes things. General, I'd like to add my team with some of yours to monitor this young man. We may be helpful," Mary said.

"Yes, it would be, specifically when the target they are presumably following is an American. I will have my people coordinate with yours," General Masoud said.

"General, have you determined the nationality of the man who was shot? Having a photo of the architect is disturbing," Mary said.

"Yes we have. He is Romanian, in Dubai apparently on a thirty-day tourist visa. He appears to be looking for work. We don't know the connection, if any, to terrorist groups or why he has a photo of the architect in his pocket," Masoud said.

"My worst suspicion is he was hired to follow the architect, by whomever we have been trying to find out. For some reason, they did not like what he was doing and shot him. If I am right, this chatter becomes very real and very sinister," the general said. The three stood up and shook hands. Mary and the major left.

In the car, Mary asked the major if he thought they should alert the architects that they may be followed.

"I don't think so, Mary, not yet. It will just confuse and complicate their plans. I recommend we wait, at least until we find out more about this young man, if he really is following them and why."

"You are right, Chuck. I will let Natalie know that she and Rusty will join the surveillance as needed. I don't want the architect to hear about the dead man with a photo of him in his pocket. If the general's assumption is correct, this changes things. These people are serious," Mary said. She picked up her cell phone and punched in Natalie's number. Natalie answered immediately. Mary brought

her up to speed about her meeting with the general and coordinating the surveillance with his people.

"I'm on my way to the safe house for an update," Mary said.

Just then, Mary's cell phone buzzed. She looked at the encrypted
name of sender; it was the deputy director, Tim Patterson. She hesitated and let it buzz a couple of times before she picked up.

"Hello, Mary. I have not heard from you since you left. I told
you I need daily reports," Tim said.

"Tim, we have been here less than a day; we are still gathering
information. I should have more to report tomorrow," Mary replied,
as her hand rolled into a fist.

"Okay, Mary. There's nothing new on this end. Don't forget to
call me tomorrow."

They both hung up, and Mary shook her head.

20

ANDY HAD A private room reserved on the business floor of the hotel for a breakfast meeting of the architects. Bob, Ayman, and Tyler Grant joined him. It was to bring Tyler up to speed, discuss CTC and the security issues, and meet with a CIA agent who requested to see them.

After introductions, they placed their orders with the waiter. Tyler was moving around the room, looking at the scenery through the large windows.

"Let us bring you up to date, Tyler. The good news is they have agreed to our proposal, including fees. In fact, we are meeting tomorrow with the technical and financial directors to finalize the contract, and we already have authorization to start work. You are coming with me," Andy said.

"That would be great. Bob gave me a copy of your proposal last week. Very impressive. I have a few questions we can go over, minor ones," Tyler said.

"That is what I was hoping you would do so we all have a clear understanding of the scope of the project. Your input is needed," Andy said.

"Tyler, technology at a very high level is what is required on this project, driven by the latest capabilities in the use of AI. That is why we were hired," Bob said.

"You should also know the expectations for this project are high, all positive," Ayman added.

"What has become clear to us is the expectations of the client go beyond designing a building; cybersecurity takes center stage," Andy said.

"That is very clear in the proposal. In fact, what you have proposed is the most sophisticated and advanced use of AI I have seen anywhere. Has anything changed?" Tyler asked.

"What has changed—maybe 'modified' is a better word—is the added emphasis upon cybersecurity with the inclusion of new, still-classified hardware, a server that is the brains of the project, to be tested first on a separate building," Andy answered.

"Well, that is an added challenge that is fascinating. I can imagine the incredible capacity needed to address all of the variables and scenarios. I assume this is why CTC is part of the team. We clearly don't have that kind of capability. Am I correct?" Tyler asked.

"No, we don't," Bob answered.

"Our challenge is we don't know if what they have or claim to have is doable. We have not seen anything yet, just assurances. You worked with CTC before, Tyler; what is your sense about their capabilities?" Andy asked.

"Well, I was involved in three projects with them, two embassies and one consulate. All involved cybersecurity. What I can tell you is they are big and well connected to the defense department and the complex defense contractors."

"Any secret-weapon stuff? Cyber weapons, if there is such a thing?" Bob asked.

"They are involved in many top-secret projects. It wouldn't surprise me if weapons research was part of it. I found them very capable and efficient. They deliver. I am detecting some concern here; what is it?"

"Tyler, you might as well know now. We have heard rumors that there may be an ulterior motive. They have promised to share every-thing about this hardware with us; in fact, it was planned for today, but they rescheduled for tomorrow," Andy said.

"Well, maybe that is all there is to it. I know them; if they said they can demonstrate what they are promising, they most probably will deliver. At least that has been my experience with them. Who are you working with from the company?" Tyler asked.

"Bill Sorenson. Do you know him?" Andy asked.

"Yes, I met him on one of the projects. Senior guy. I found him to be quite decent and professional."

"You may be right, Tyler. In the meantime, we have some entity out there determined that we are planning to install a powerful weapon in Dubai directed at them. In fact, I was contacted by a CIA agent; she wanted to meet with us to give us some kind of detail about some of her concerns. She should be here in about half an hour. I asked her to come up to the business floor," Andy said.

"CIA? Wow, this is getting serious. I must tell my daughter; she is into all the spy stuff," Tyler said, generating laughter.

Like clockwork, half an hour later, the hostess opened the door, and two women walked in. The four men stood up, waiting for introductions.

"Good morning, gentlemen. I am Mary Tobias with the CIA, and this is my team leader, Natalie Arseniev. Pleasure to meet you."

"Pleasure meeting you, Mary, Natalie. I am Andy Sykes, the project director. This is STR architect Bob Thornton, who is my boss; Tyler Grant, who just joined us; and Ayman Noury, president of his Dubai architectural firm and of the team."

"It is nice meeting you all. Congratulations for winning this Al Bustan project. You must be very pleased, a great win," Mary said.

"Thank you, Mary. It is not every day that we meet someone from the CIA. I am not sure if we should be excited or afraid," Andy added with a smile.

"Well, now you have. From all that I have heard, it should be a great project. Your reputation is well-known and well deserved. My purpose for meeting with you today is to share some potential worrisome aspects of this project and also to learn more from you about the project. I am sure you are aware of the interest of the US and the UAE governments in its cybersecurity. Both governments are hoping this new hardware can deliver positive results," Mary said. "We are here at the request of national security. There are rumors that the cybersecurity proposed is not a defensive measure against cyberattacks but potentially an offensive weapon aimed directly at neutralizing electronic capabilities." Mary stopped for a minute, looking for a reaction.

"We—UAE security and the CIA—don't know how real the threat is. Their fear, legitimate or not, is driving the determination to destroy this weapon, whatever it may be or wherever it is located," Mary said.

"Mary, with all due respect, we have been given assurances by the technology drivers, CTC, that what is being proposed is advanced and sophisticated hardware, a server, approved by both governments. That assurance was given to us and to the CEO of Pinnacle Enterprises. They assured us that the system would be clearly and transparently identified to us very soon. We demanded it once we heard about the secrecy around all this," Bob answered.

"Furthermore, we have not yet signed a contract. Nothing has been planned or designed. So where and why do they suspect the threat?" Andy added.

"Here is the deal. They suspect this weapons system, whatever it is, is already here and that installation has begun in some unknown location. It is not finalized; that is where you come in. Something about your programming skill is needed to finalize it. We don't know what that is," Mary said.

"To read between the lines, since they don't know what and where this weapon is," Andy paused, "we are the target. Is that what I am hearing?"

"Unfortunately, that is what we believe. That is why we, as well as security here, have assigned people to follow you as a precaution," Mary said.

"Mary, what are you trying to tell us?" Bob asked.

"Be cautious. Call me anytime you see or hear something that is worrisome or threatening. Don't get me wrong; the project is real. Pinnacle is a highly respected company. It may be nothing, or there may be rogue activities taking place. We intend to find out. We will continue to have our agents keep an eye on you and others on your team. We don't want to take any chances."

"Mary, you can imagine what this means to us. We are architects. We design and create. We build communities where people live and work. We have a strong company culture of integrity and responsibility. Working with the CIA is not what we signed up for. It's awkward at best. We are not spies; we don't operate in secrecy. We appreciate what you are telling us, but please understand there are some lines we cannot cross," Bob said.

"Understood. We are the necessary nuisance. You are not the first and won't be the last to feel this way about the CIA. Just remember, we have enemies that want to do us harm. Our job is to do what needs to be done to protect America and Americans. We are not asking you to spy for us. We are informing you of the potential dangers, how we can help, and for you to be very cautious until we get to the bottom of this. One more thing," she added. "Are you satisfied that the hardware being proposed can produce the desired results?"

"Not yet. We are scheduled to meet with CTC tomorrow, hopefully to receive the briefing we asked for," Andy said.

"Okay. Please let me know if you hear or see anything unusual. I will stay in touch; here is my cell number. Call me. I am available twenty-four/seven." Mary and Natalie shook hands with them and were ready to leave, when Jennifer walked in.

"Hi, guys," Jennifer greeted Andy and Bob. "I thought I would crash your party and have a late breakfast with you."

"Mary, Natalie, please meet my wife, Jennifer, the party crasher. Jennifer, Mary and Natalie are with the CIA. They are here to arrest you. Just kidding. Some bad guys think we may be working on some secret project. How was your walk?" Andy said.

"Great. What a city. I am going up to the room. I was kidding about breakfast. I just wanted to say hello. Mary, Natalie, nice to meet you both. See you all later."

"Jennifer, it's wonderful to meet you. We were leaving too," Mary said. She and Natalie followed Jennifer and left the room.

21

ELIAS DROVE HIMSELF to the warehouse where Bill told him to meet. The black box was in the warehouse, secure, Bill assured him. He had a lot of doubts about Bill and all his promises and assurances. He wasn't sure how effective and reliable Bill was.

Bill was waiting in his car when Elias arrived. They both walked from their cars and proceeded toward the warehouse. From outside, it looked abandoned, with broken glass windows and trash strewn outside.

"What is this place? Are you sure it is secure?" Elias asked.

"Yes, it is; you'll see," Bill answered.

"What if the box is discovered or stolen and experts could determine its true purpose?"

"They can't. It is useless to them until such time when it is programmed, and integration with the censors is completed," Bill said.

"Okay, Bill," Elias said as he looked around and shook his head. "Are you sure this is a safe place to hide such an important piece of equipment? This doesn't give me much comfort."

"No worries, Elias. This place is very safe," Bill said as he pulled out a keychain.

Bill had a key for one of the entry doors. He walked in, and Elias followed. The warehouse was dark. No lights except for the daylight through the windows.

Bill had a flashlight. They walked halfway through the warehouse, when Bill found a light switch and flipped it on. A corner of the warehouse lit up. There was not much of anything special except for a couple of benches and a few overused chairs.

There was one door, which Bill opened. He turned on the switch. It was a room full of abandoned furniture. Bill walked to the furthest corner of the room. Nothing there but concrete walls.

"Behind this wall is our black box, very well hidden," Bill said.

"There is nothing but concrete walls," Elias said.

"You will see." Bill went to the corner and moved approximately four feet away. He started to gently tap on a small area of the wall. In a few seconds, a pop sounded, and a four-inch square, what appeared to be a part of the concrete wall, popped open.

Bill opened the small cover, and there was a keyhole. He took a key from his chain, inserted it in the hole, and turned. A section of the concrete approximately three feet wide started opening very slowly.

When the door was wide open, Bill motioned to Elias. "Here we go, Elias. Let's go get the black box."

They walked into a very small room, no more than six feet square. "What is this? Is this a joke?" Elias shouted.

The room was completely empty.

"What the hell is the meaning of this? You'd better explain and explain fast," Elias demanded.

"I don't know. I swear. I checked this two days ago. It was here. I am as puzzled as you are," Bill said.

"Puzzled? Puzzled? Are you kidding me? You'd better panic, my friend. If you don't have an explanation and if you have lost the box, you know what that means. You know what will happen to you." Elias was furious.

"Okay, Elias. Let's get out of here first and talk outside. I don't know yet what is going on, but I will figure it out." Bill walked out, and Elias followed.

Once outside, with no one around, Elias looked at Bill. "Alright, what's going on?" he said.

"First, Elias, we have not lost the box. The box is safe," Bill said.

"Bill, I don't have time for riddles." Elias was getting impatient.

"Elias, what was in there was not the real box. It was a decoy," Bill said.

Elias didn't know whether he should punch him or feel relieved.

"Okay, Bill, explain. This better be good." Elias tried to remain calm.

"I have the real black box hidden in a very secure place. I created a duplicate, identical to this, and placed it in this secret place, just in case," Bill said.

"Just in case what?" Elias demanded.

Bill hesitated. He looked at Elias, growing more impatient. "I did it to protect myself, Elias."

"Protect from whom? From me?" Elias could not believe this.

"No, Elias, not from you. From my partners in the US."

"Enough. Bill, it is time you come clean. What the hell is going on?" Elias screamed.

"I have partners, powerful partners. I told you I did. This black box is my security if everything falls apart. If that happens, I will be left alone holding the bag. I will be the fall guy."

"Wait a minute. If that is all true, where is the real box? More importantly, who took this box? How did they know?" Elias asked, fuming. "Have you shared these locations with anybody?"

"Jesus, I haven't thought about that. Only one other person knows. Only the location of this box, not the other," Bill replied.

"Who?" Elias said.

"I can't tell you, not now," Bill said.

22

MARY AND NATALIE went back to the safe house, where Natalie said, "Rusty and the local team have spotted and are tracking the young man who they believe was following Andy. They saw him at the coffee shop once with an older woman, and they are to report back on their progress. There were no other meetings that they saw. The young man and the older woman seemed to go separate ways in different destinations." Still, both agreed that they would continue the surveillance.

"Mary, I did hear back from my friend at the Department of Defense," Natalie added.

"What did you find out?"

"She told me that anything CTC has designed to be used to defend against cyberattacks through hacking or other means is well-known by the Defense Department and other security agencies. They are closely tied to defense. The question we need answered is if we have the technology that can turn this hardware defensive capability into an offensive cyber weapon, as the rumors seem to suggest."

"And do we?" Mary asked.

"I was told we do," Natalie replied.

23

I T WAS AN old twenty-story apartment building in a working-class area, with narrow and crowded alleys where Natalie's team was monitoring. She was in the coffee shop around the corner, watching and waiting to hear from Rusty. They were monitoring the apartment building's front entrance. They had observed, over the last few days, the young man entering the building at least twice, and this time they spotted the older lady going in earlier than him. They assumed the building may be a meeting place.

Natalie had two other local members stationed in Dubai assisting in the surveillance. Her cell phone buzzed; it was Rusty. "We plan to send one of our people inside. They have a clerk stationed at the reception desk. We will try to see if we can get some information. The two suspects have been inside for over an hour. There has to be something going on."

"Let me know what you find out," Natalie said.

There was a sense of urgency that something was about to happen, though they were not sure what or when. Natalie knew they could not move too quickly and alert the terrorists. It was essential to be certain. No guesswork.

The local team member was an Emirati, and that was how he was dressed. He entered the building carrying a gift-wrapped package. He walked directly to the reception desk, where a young Indian man was sitting.

The Emirati approached the security clerk and told him, "I have a birthday gift from my uncle to be delivered to a young man and his aunt who live in the building." He was very apologetic that he lost the paper with the names and apartment unit number. "But I can't go back to my uncle; he would be very upset." He begged the guard to help him look at the names of the renters and hopefully he could find the right one.

The guard said, "I can't do that. It is against the rules, and I'd be fired if the owners found out." He assured the Emirati that it would not happen, but the hundred *dirhams* was very helpful to smooth the way. The guard looked around and slipped the note in his pocket.

He started looking at the roster of unit renters and found what may be the best fit. "It's a unit on the twelfth floor, rented to an older woman living alone. A young man visits her from time to time. But I cannot give you the unit number because they are not there."

That was a surprise. They were watching the building and did not see either of the two leave.

"Are you sure?" the CIA agent asked.

"Yes," said the guard. "I saw them leave separately. They came down the unit elevators and entered the parking garage elevators. This is an older building. Only one elevator goes down to the garage."

"That's okay. I can just go up and quickly leave the gift in the room."

"I can't do that. I can't leave my desk," the guard said.

"That's fine. Just give me the key. I will be up, leave the gift with a note, and be back down before anybody can find out," the agent said as he slipped him another hundred *dirhams*.

The guard hesitated, looked around, and then slipped the money in his pocket. He took out a key and said, "Unit 1202. Be quick."

The agent took the key and went up to unit 1202. Ten minutes later, he was back down without the gift, thanked the guard, gave him his key back, and left.

The agent went directly to where Rusty was and told him, "The apartment was stark, just basic minimal furnishings, very clean, no clutter. I took pictures of the apartment and managed to get rid of the gift-wrapped box in the garbage shoot by the elevators. I found a fingerprint on the door handle."

Rusty called Natalie to let her know what happened. They had completely ignored the garage entrance. He sent the photo of the unit to Natalie, who asked him to have the agent check the cameras in the garage. The time was narrowed to one hour, which could give the team the make of the car and license plates. Rusty said, "I'll follow up, but I'm not sure if the old building has cameras in the garage."

24

HANIA PICKED UP Jennifer at the hotel for lunch and a visit to a museum. Jennifer was scheduled to go back to the United States the following evening for work; this was to be a farewell lunch before she left.

Hania had planned the visit to the national museum; she told Jennifer it was worth seeing. Islamic and UAE history followed by lunch in a restaurant adjacent to the museum. They were both aware of the black SUV following them with two security men in the front seat, as Andy had told them earlier.

Jennifer and Hania had become fast friends. They were kindred spirits: independent, adventurous, and highly educated. They shared curiosity about the world and the passion to explore. Both enjoyed humor and had a magnetic laugh.

As they were leaving the hotel, a man who was in the lobby reading the *Khaleej Times* put down his paper and walked outside. He casually lit a cigarette and then pulled out his cell phone. He was laughing and talking as the car with Hania driving and Jennifer in the front seat began leaving the hotel, followed by a black SUV with two men in front. The man in front of the hotel expertly snapped photos of each of the vehicles, with a cigarette in one hand and without being noticed. He sent them to his three contacts, stationed at different locations along the route to the museum and waiting for his signal.

Two blocks from the museum, Jennifer and Hania, laughing and sharing stories, did not notice that the black SUV was not following them. Just as they turned the corner, an unmarked white van intercepted them, almost hitting their car. Another van blocked their retreat. A third unmarked white van drove next to the passenger side, and three masked men jumped out with guns pointed at Hania and Jennifer. One of them ordered Jennifer to release her seatbelt, and she obeyed, shaking.

The three men were dressed in black with black ski masks on. They were tall and lean. The one pointing the gun at Jennifer pulled her out of the car, immediately covered her head with a black hood, and shoved her into the white van, where a second masked man tied her hands and legs and placed tape over her mouth. The man with the gun was already back in the van, driving away. The other two vans left the scene at a high speed. The three vehicles went in different directions.

Hania started screaming; she opened her door and jumped out just as the two security men arrived and were out of their SUV, rushing toward her. She was in shock and pointing in the direction where she thought the abductors had gone. One agent was on his car phone contacting his superior at headquarters. He was told to stay on the line while General Masoud was informed. The superior was back in less than a minute. "Stay there and wait for other agents to arrive and interview pedestrians who may have seen what happened." He also instructed the other agent to drive Hania back to headquarters.

———

General Masoud picked up his phone and called Ayman to let him know what happened. "Come to headquarters to join your wife when she arrives; she is in shock." Ayman screamed and then asked if Andy had been told. "No. I'm going to ask Mary to do that. Do not share the information about the kidnapping with anyone for now."

———

"Oh, no . . . oh, no. How? When?" Mary said when she received the news from the general.

"Mary, I have my team mobilized on the ground, and we are reviewing the cameras. For now, I want you to let Andy, the husband, know and assure him we will get his wife back unharmed. Other than that, keep this quiet." Mary said she would and then rushed out the door in the safe house, pointing for Natalie to join her.

———

Andy was in the hotel lobby with Bob and Tyler when his cell phone rang. It was Ayman.

"Andy," Ayman said. He was crying, shaken. "Jennifer. It's Jennifer . . . she has been kidnapped."

Andy dropped the phone and slumped to the ground.

Bob picked up the cell phone. "Hello, this is Bob. Who is this? What is going on?"

"Bob, Jennifer has been abducted," Ayman said, sobbing.

"How? Where? She was with Hania. They had security people protecting them. What the hell happened?" Bob was shouting.

Tyler got up, also shaken, and tried to comfort Andy. After listening to Ayman, Bob joined them and put his arm around Andy.

"What happened, Bob? Is Jennifer hurt?" Andy asked, shaken, unsure. He grabbed Bob's arm and would not let go.

"We don't know yet, Andy. We don't know for sure what happened," Bob said.

"Damn it, I should have known and not let her go out. This is all my fault." Andy stood up, not sure what to do. "Bob, we have to get her back. Do you hear me? We have to get her back!"

Just as Andy was getting the attention of the people in the lobby, Mary and Natalie showed up, rushing into the hotel. Mary sensed immediately that Andy already knew his wife was kidnapped. She grabbed him by the arm, with Natalie beside her.

"We will get her back, Andy. I promise you we will get her back. For now, let's all go up to the suite. We'll work from there. Andy, Andy, give me your room key," Mary said, taking charge.

As they all headed to the elevators, Mary's cell phone buzzed; it was the general. "Hania is extremely emotional, but she managed to give me the details of what happened." His vast security apparatus had already gone into full mobilization, checking street cameras and questioning his security people and any bystanders who may have seen something. Mary conveyed the message to Andy.

In Andy's suite, Natalie was on her phone talking to her team. Mary sat next to Andy and placed her arm around him, assuring him that they would get Jennifer back.

"Andy, those kidnappers are not after Jennifer. They will not harm her. They are after you. At some point soon, they will contact you, most probably using Jennifer's cell phone. We will just have to wait here until then. In the meantime, the UAE security and our team are following up on all leads. Every detail will be covered. Every lead will be followed. Andy, we will get Jennifer back. I promise you."

"Alright," Andy said after a long pause, collecting his thoughts and emotions and trying very hard to switch to crisis management mode. He stood up, unsure of himself, and held his head with both hands. He tried to say something but only muttered incoherent words. He went to the bar and drank a glass of water and then leaned over the bar and started rocking back and forth.

"I am the target. I know that," he said as he straightened up. "They will call me. They have to. What they want from me, I'm not sure yet, but I will find out. In the meantime, I don't want any moves of any kind by security people or anybody else that places Jennifer in harm's way. Absolutely no move, nothing, without my approval."

"Andy, I promise you nothing will happen that in any way may harm Jennifer. You must trust me. I have dealt with these kinds of situations and with people like that."

"Who do you think these people are? Terrorists, Al Qaida, Iran? What do they want? I have nothing to give them. This is awful, just awful," Andy said.

"We don't know. My feeling is this might be state-sponsored, probably Iranian. It is too sophisticated an operation to be otherwise, which is good." She was trying to comfort Andy.

Andy started pacing again; the anguish on his face was stark. He was pacing aimlessly, like a panicked and lost stranger. Bob tried to comfort him, not sure what to say.

"They can't hurt her; they just can't hurt her," Andy said, staring at Mary.

"They won't, Andy; they won't. They need her to get to you. They will not harm her," Mary said.

"Why didn't they just kidnap me?" he asked.

"They probably thought you were guarded too well."

"Okay, what do we do now?" Andy said.

"On this end, we wait. The general and his team are in high-alert mode; they will come up with something very soon, I am convinced."

25

MARY CALLED GENERAL Masoud, and he told her they were review-ing the street cameras where the kidnapping took place. "We should have some answers fairly quickly. How is Andy doing?"

"As well as can be expected," she said.

"It is just Natalie, Bob and I in with Andy," she said. Masoud told her he'd call if they found any clues.

The room was quiet, and all eyes were on Andy. Mary went back to him; he was shaken but under control, impatiently waiting for the phone call. Mary asked Natalie if she heard back from Rusty.

"He's reviewing the camera tapes of the apartment building garage with Masoud's people. They'll let us know soon if they find anything."

Bob asked if he could call his partners back in LA. "No," Mary told him. "For now, total silence." Masoud had also told her that none of this could hit the press; he demanded a total news blackout. Mary said she'd have to call the director of the CIA within the hour. "He can't hear it from other sources." Masoud agreed. He had done the same.

"Mary?" Andy stood up. "Any idea when and how they will try to reach me?"

"These situations are never the same. They vary. My hunch is they will be calling you sooner rather than later. They have already made their point. They are professionals. They know that we, the

CIA, are engaged, so it will not be long. They also know the sophisticated security in this country will not take long to find them, no matter how good they are."

"Is there any chance the kidnappers are not Iranians? Maybe Russians or Russian-directed?" Bob asked.

"Good question, but we simply don't know yet," Mary replied.

"Wait a minute, Mary." Natalie stepped in. "What if it is not Iranians, but whoever the kidnappers are want us to believe they are Iranians. There are all kinds of reasons they would do that."

"I had thought about that; it's a distinct possibility," Mary said. "I can't imagine any of our adversaries would do this. Neither the Russians nor the Chinese would take that kind of risk and make such provocations. Terrorist groups lack this kind of precision. That leaves allies. I can't think of one that would want to do this, though. For what purpose?" Mary was still digesting the possibility.

Mary's cell buzzed. It was Rusty. "There's nothing on the tapes of the garage. The older woman and the young man left fifteen minutes apart, according to the apartment security clerk. I did go back to the apartment with the team to try to find DNA samples. There was one empty glass in the bathroom, which we took with us to be tested. The fingerprint on the door was also given to the lab."

Mary hung up and told the others that she was going to the other room to call the director. She went to the small kitchenette and dialed the number on her secure cell phone. It rang three times before the director picked up the phone.

"It is three in the morning. This better be good," he said.

"Sir, sorry to be bothering you at this hour, but you need to know. Jennifer, the wife of the architect, who appears to be the key to all this, was kidnapped early this afternoon. Our team is working closely with the national security team to determine who did it and why," Mary said.

"Now you have my full attention. Hold on for a minute while I go to the study and check the messages regarding this, if any." She could hear him go into his private and secure study and turn on his computer. "Okay, Mary, what is your take on who may be behind this?"

"For now, we are assuming it is Iranians, but that's just a guess. The operation is too professional and sophisticated to be a terrorist group. Jennifer, the kidnapped wife, had security men right behind her in another car. There were other security people waiting at her destination. We don't think it can be the Russians or Chinese. They are too smart to pull something like this," she said.

"What's the plan?" he asked.

"We are waiting for the phone call from the kidnappers. I think they are using his wife to get to the architect. Security is looking at the cameras all around the blocks where the kidnapping took place."

"Okay, Mary. What do you need at this end?"

"For now, we have a complete news blackout until we know more. I am not ruling out internal leaks or even participation."

"Understood. Keep me informed." The director hung up.

Mary went back to the sitting room, where the others were. No news yet. No phone calls either.

"Did you inform the deputy director?" Natalie asked.

"I called the director. I'm sure I will be hearing about this from the deputy. I'll call him in a few hours, but I don't need his meddling right now."

26

JENNIFER WAS BLINDFOLDED. She had no idea where she was. All she recalled was that the ride with the abductors took about ten minutes from the moment she was moved to a different car. They had removed the hood and the gag in her mouth but not the blindfold or the ropes.

She played the sequence of events in her head repeatedly. It all happened so quickly, with such precision. None of her captors had uttered a word. She wasn't sure how many there were. She also determined that she was not in a high-rise building. She had heard the sound of a garage door opening, the van driving through, and the garage door closing.

The van door had slid open, and she was pulled out. She remembered they were not rough in handling her. *Who are these kidnappers? What do they want?* She knew that she would be the bait to get Andy.

She heard the door open. Someone had come inside, walking toward her. She felt a hand remove the ropes tying her feet and then her blindfold. She opened her eyes. The room was dark; she adjusted her eyes, straining to see. The room appeared to be clean but stark. She was sitting on a couch, and there were only two chairs, a wooden desk, and a small refrigerator in the corner next to a sink. She also saw a door at the other end, probably a bathroom. No windows. Air conditioning working. Comfortable.

A young woman in Western attire with a hijab covering most of her face, except for her eyes, walked in. She had managed to hide her identity well. "Hello, Mrs. Sykes. My job is to make sure you are comfortable. I am sure you do not want to be here. You want to be with your husband. That is our desire also," she said. "We have a refrigerator with water, juices, snacks. I have made tea for you. Let me know if you would like some coffee."

"Where am I? Why have I been kidnapped?" Jennifer wanted to stay calm. The young woman did not answer. "Please tell me if my husband has been contacted, if he knows I am safe." Again, no response.

"What is your name?" Jennifer tried another approach.

"Amina. Just call me Amina."

"Amina, why am I here? What do you want? I am sure whatever it is, you can work it out with my husband." Jennifer tried again. Amina did not answer.

"Can I talk to someone in authority? I may be of help to clear up things for you," Jennifer said.

"In due time, Mrs. Sykes," Amina said as she walked out of the room.

27

GENERAL MASOUD WAS in the control room with his specialists. Rusty was there also. They were looking at the various tapes located at the intersections. What became very clear was that everything was perfectly synchronized. No room for error.

It was obvious the kidnappers knew the street pattern very well. They knew when and how to strike. They had timed it to anticipate turns and traffic lights.

They saw the front car with Hania driving and Jennifer in the passenger side. The black SUV with the two security guards was close behind. Out of nowhere, this white van slipped between the two cars, just as the front car turned right. The van stopped just in time for the light to turn red. The security car was trapped.

Within seconds of the front car with Hania and Jennifer turning, another white van intercepted and blocked them. They saw a third van immediately pull up next to the passenger side. Three masked men jumped out, guns drawn; they opened the passenger door, yanked Jennifer out, and pushed her into the van.

The whole thing took less than two minutes. All three vans sped away. By the time the security car arrived, everyone was gone, except for Hania, who appeared to be in total shock.

They followed the path of the vans through the street cameras. The three went in opposite directions. Each one moved to busy intersections within a few blocks of the scene. Then all three went into underground parking garages. None appeared to have left the garages.

General Masoud ordered all of the three garage cameras to be brought up. They saw all three vans entering the different garages. Each one was visible and tracked upon entry. After the entry level, all cameras on the main parking levels, including the exit, were blank.

It was obvious that the cameras were somehow deactivated. It was also assumed that all three vans were abandoned and left in the garages. "There must have been getaway vans or cars in the garages waiting for them," Rusty surmised. The general ordered that all three garages be searched and the vans confiscated and searched for clues.

General Masoud picked up his cell phone and punched in Mary's number. She picked up right away, and he told her what they had found.

"Mary, this was an extremely sophisticated and professional operation. The timing for each move had to be absolutely perfect to be able to do this," he said. "In my opinion, to execute this operation would require a large team with sophisticated technology; the other possible alternative or addition is they had knowledge of the route in advance. What I am trying to say is they must have had advance information about where Jennifer and Hania were going, what time and what route." The general was direct.

Mary was silent. The implication of what the general was saying was enormous. This meant that someone in the very small inner circle must be working with the kidnappers.

"Mary, we managed to identify the older woman from our surveillance cameras. We found a match in our data banks. She's a nurse in a local hospital. Hospital officials said she called in sick this morning. We have her home address. A team went to locate her, but she wasn't there. We have a citywide net trying to locate her. Her name is Selma Hamdi; she is Syrian and has been in Dubai close to five years."

"How about the young man?"

"Nothing yet. No fingerprints. No DNA. No matches."

"I'm still trying to absorb what you were saying regarding the insider involvement. I know the team well. Can't imagine who it might be. We also have to consider other possibilities, such as people with Pinnacle Enterprises and also someone within your security team," Mary said.

"Mary, I agree; we have to look at all possibilities. Not only who executed the operation but for whom. First step is who had access to the information. We should have more to share; we will continue the search for the older woman and our on-the-ground investigations. In the meantime, let's stay in close touch," the general said, and they both hung up.

Mary went back to the group. Nothing had happened there. No phone calls. She did not share her conversation with the general.

Mary started thinking of who may have leaked the information and was, by definition, part of the plot. But first she needed to know for certain who had knowledge of the destination and the route that Jennifer and Hania took. In her mind, the list included Hania and her husband, Andy and his wife, and the two architects Bob and Tyler, who were with Andy all morning. She also included General Masoud's security team and her own team. *Anyone else?* She kept thinking. *How about Pinnacle? How about Cyber Technologies?*

Mary went to Andy and sat next to him. "Andy, we will get Jennifer back safely. I promise you. I just have a couple of questions to help me understand what happened better. Who knew where Jennifer and Hania were going? Do you know if they had reservations? These are purely routine questions."

Andy sat up. He was thinking, partly to answer Mary and partly to figure out why she was asking the question in the first place. "Mary. I think I know why you are asking the question. You think somebody on our side may be working with them. Is that right? I need to know." Andy was insistent.

"Yes, Andy, we believe that may be a possibility. We have to look at all options. We cannot ignore it. We may conclude there wasn't any leak from our side, but we can't take the risk. We are looking at our team, the security team assigned to this, and possible contacts made. Everything."

"Okay, I understand. The only people who knew where they were going, when, and how to get there were Hania and Ayman, and possibly Bob and Tyler; they may have overheard our conversations. They were in the lobby with us. That leaves security people and anyone that Ayman or Hania may have shared with accidentally. I did not tell anybody."

"We will interview everyone on our list. To let you know, national security is looking at all relevant street cameras. We should have some conclusions soon."

Mary stood up and motioned to Natalie to join her in the other room. She brought Natalie up to date and told her to join Rusty at the national security headquarters. "I want an assessment of what is happening there from your perspective. Report back to me. I'll stay close to Andy."

28

BILL SORENSON WAS alone in his hotel room. He sat still, staring at the wall. The events of the last twenty-four hours had turned his life upside down. He felt alone.

The disappearance of the black box was very troublesome. *Who knew about this? How could they get in without a key?* He was shaken. More than that, he was frightened.

Only one person knew about the location of the fake box. He knew how to get in. What that person did not know was that there was another box. The box functioned just as the real box did. It looked and functioned perfectly, but it had a key component missing: the program to enable it to become an offensive cyber weapon.

Only one person knew.

And now Andy's wife is kidnapped in one of the most secure cities on earth. To be able to pull off something like this with such precision and audacity requires a very sophisticated organization. Who? Who is capable?

It is not the Iranians. It can't be. Maybe. Who knows? Oh, God, what have I done? How am I getting out of this? He knew he could not call anyone; his only option was to leverage what he had and what he knew—if he could. He stood up, started pacing, and then walked over to the bar and poured himself a drink of scotch. He took a large gulp, set the glass down, and started pacing again, his breathing strained. He sat down again, holding his face with both hands, his breathing faster and shallower.

He knew, sooner or later, that internal security and the CIA would make the connection to him. Neither of his two cell phones nor his hotel ground line would be secure. He decided to connect with Jason, his team member, to feel him out and see what he knew.

He texted and asked him to come to his suite immediately. Jason responded that he was on his way. Bill waited for him, not knowing what Jason knew, uncertain if he could trust him.

When Jason arrived, Bill had coffee made and offered him a cup. Bill asked Jason, "Is there anything new going on? Any rumors?"

Jason looked at Bill, disheveled and stressed. "Nothing unusual," he said.

Bill stood up and started pacing again, his movements erratic.

"Bill, what's wrong? What is going on?" Jason asked.

"What I am about to share with you is extremely confidential. I have not shared it yet with headquarters. I need your word," Bill stressed.

"Of course, Bill. Absolutely."

"Alright. Earlier today, Jennifer Sykes, the wife of Andy Sykes, lead architect for the team, was kidnapped." Bill was still pacing.

"What? You have got to be kidding. This is unbelievable. How can that happen?" Jason said, stunned.

"I don't know; it is a shock."

"Who would do that? Bill, this has to be related to Al Bustan. That means us, Bill. You have to let the main office know. They cannot hear it from the *New York Times*," Jason said, leaning forward.

"Right now, security has a tight lid on this. We can't afford to be the leak. They would demand to know how we found out. All kinds of questions would follow," Bill said.

"How *did* you find out?"

"Elias Khoury, the CEO of Pinnacle, told me."

"What do we do now? You know we are vulnerable. Once they

start their questioning and probing, they will be coming after us. I am surprised they haven't yet. What do we do?" Jason asked.

"Have you been reporting back to headquarters?" Bill asked.

"Yes, routine stuff," Jason said.

"Okay. For now, keep it that way. I expect I will be contacted by security and/or the CIA any time now. You may be too. Remember, we are not accused or guilty of anything," Bill said.

Jason said he would. As he stood up to leave, he noticed Bill pacing again, holding a cocktail.

———

As soon as he was back in his room, Jason picked up his secure cell phone and punched in the US number. The person on the other end picked up immediately. Jason shared what Bill just told him and asked for instructions.

"Locate the servers and make sure they are protected."

Jason restated that he didn't know where they were. "Bill was very guarded and had not shared the location."

"Keep pushing. It's critical that you retrieve the boxes."

———

Bill sat down with his glass of scotch in his hand. He was frozen, gazing at the blank wall in his suite. He took his jacket off and then his tie and threw them on the couch. He picked up his cell phone and dialed a number; it took a few rings before a woman answered.

"Bill, is that you? It is early in the morning. Are you okay? You never call me at this hour. Is everything okay?"

"Everything is fine, Helen. It has been a long day, I miss you; just wanted to hear your voice. Are the kids alright?" Bill said.

"We are fine, Bill, just fine. I miss you too. Are you sure you are okay?" Helen asked.

"Yes, of course. Just wanted to hear your voice," Bill said and hung up.

29

"**I AM CONCERNED,**" **MARY** said on her cell phone. "Andy has not been contacted. The longer this goes on, the more volatile the situation, Jennifer's safety becomes questionable. The kidnappers must know that in Dubai, time is not on their side. Sooner or later, the press will find out, especially the longer this drags on. The whole game changes once that happens." She was looking at Andy on the other side of the room, pacing and deep in thought. She knew he was blaming himself. He was in great pain, trying hard to keep his composure. "Any new development on your end?"

"Security has located Selma, the older woman. She has been arrested and brought into headquarters. General Masoud has asked me to join the interrogation team. It will be starting in fifteen minutes," Natalie said.

"How about the young man?" Mary asked.

"Nothing yet. No signs of him so far."

"Okay, Natalie. Give me a call as soon as you find out anything. Doesn't matter how small or irrelevant." Mary ended the call.

She started to join Andy and Bob, when her cell phone buzzed again. It was the deputy director of the CIA, her immediate superior.

"Mary, you should have called me first before you called the director. I should not be hearing it from him. I thought I made this very clear to you," Tim Patterson, the deputy director of the CIA, said. He was angry, almost screaming at her.

"The press will get a hold of this, if they haven't already. Once that happens, we lose control. The finger pointing will start. We will be crucified. I can see the headlines: 'The CIA Knew All about This.' We knew they were in harm's way, yet we could not protect them. They will have a field day. Mary, you know, we may have one day, possibly two, three if we're lucky, before the press finds out. Are we any closer to rescuing Mrs. Sykes?"

"Tim, everyone is on it. We are making progress. No resolution yet. We all know that time is not on our side. So must the kidnappers, as sophisticated as they may be," Mary said.

"I am assuming the kidnapping has to be directly related to the Al Bustan cyber defense. Any new developments regarding the chatter?" Tim asked.

"We were moving on that track quite well when this kidnapping happened. I am sorry, Tim, about not communicating with you first. It will not happen again," Mary said, knowing full well it was a promise that she most likely could not keep. It wasn't just her way; it was a direct command by the director.

Mary hung up and went over to see Andy. Bob had ordered sandwiches. Andy was sitting quietly but hadn't eaten. Mary sat by him. "How are you holding up, Andy?" she asked.

"Why haven't they called? Doesn't sound good, does it?" he said. He was very worried, almost in a panic.

"Andy, they will. They cannot and will not hurt Jennifer. It is you they want. Now, one more time. Why do they need you? It is your expertise, obviously. What is that exactly? Please, Andy, Bob, share that with me. If we know the details, we could have a clearer path to get this solved and bring Jennifer back. What is it they want from you?"

"It is the hardware, the server. It has to be. Somehow they must think that Andy has it and he has to exchange it for Jennifer. They probably will demand that Andy make it operational." Bob said.

"That is where we come in. According to CTC, the server's

capabilities are significantly enhanced by the added capacity we provide in placing sensors and processors throughout the building connected remotely to the server."

"What good is this without a server and without a building to implement it?" Mary asked.

"What value we can provide right now is none. That is the problem. Without this server, super box, or whatever it is, we are blind. We are worthless." Bob stopped, searching for answers.

"So without the server, you are of no help. I know you haven't seen it. Where is it? They must think it is here in Dubai. Could that be true?" Mary said.

"It is in Dubai; CTC has it. They were scheduled to walk us through it. We insisted they do, but they only shared the codes that activate the server and enable the programming. We are still waiting to see the server," Andy said as he stood up.

"You are absolutely right, Mary. They must believe the box is here and that we have it. Why would they go through this highly risky and elaborate scheme if it wasn't?" Bob added.

"If it is here, where is it? Who has it?" Mary jumped in.

"The only person who would know is Bill Sorenson of Cyber Technologies," Andy chimed in, fully engaged.

"Okay. It is time I have a talk with Mr. Sorenson. I have his number." Mary punched in the number for Bill Sorenson. "Mr. Sorenson, my name is Mary Tobias."

"I know who you are. I was expecting your call," Bill answered. "Don't leave your hotel. I will be there in ten minutes."

30

NATALIE WAS IN the interrogation room. There were two national security officers, a man and a woman. The man would do the questioning, and the woman would interpret for Natalie, who had some understanding of Arabic.

Selma, a shy, frail woman who appeared to be in her sixties, was brought in. She did not match the profile of a terrorist or kidnapper, but appearances can be deceiving. Natalie had known many who did not fit the profile of a terrorist. She could tell life had not been kind to Selma. Sadness and resignation were evident under the hijab covering her hair.

"Give us your full name, please," the interrogator asked in a calm and kind manner.

"My name is Selma Hamdi."

"Where were you born?"

"I was born in Aleppo, Syria."

"How old are you?"

"I am fifty-three years old," she said. Natalie was taken aback. She looked at least ten years older.

"When did you come to Dubai?"

"I think it was five years ago."

"Why did you come to Dubai?"

"Our home was destroyed. My husband and my two daughters

were killed in bombing raids. My nephew was the only family member left. We came to Dubai to find a job."

"How did you survive? Who helped you?"

"I have a cousin who has been living here for many years and helped me find a job as a nurse and my nephew as a waiter in one of the hotels."

"What is your cousin's name, and where does he live?"

"His name is Yahia Saleh. He lives in Sharjah."

The interrogator pointed to the two-way mirror, gesturing to follow up on the cousin. "What is your nephew's name, and where is he?"

Selma hesitated. She looked at the interrogator, pleading. "He is a very good boy, has never done anything bad," she said.

"I am sure he is. But we need to talk to him. He will be fine as long as you tell us the truth. What is his name, and where can we find him?"

"His name is Ali Hamza. He lives with me. He is looking for work now," Selma said.

"Now, Selma, I want you to listen to me very carefully. I am going to ask you questions. You must answer me truthfully. No harm will come to you if you do. But if you don't, you and your nephew and your cousin will go to prison and get deported. Do you understand what I am saying to you?" The interrogator leaned forward, staring at her intimidatingly.

Selma broke down and started sobbing. The interrogator offered her tissue paper, and she wiped the tears. She was quiet for a few minutes. The interrogator waited. She finally looked up and straightened up with surprising dignity, not defiance.

"Yes, sir, please go ahead and ask me what you want to know. I don't lie. I will tell the truth," she said.

"Thank you, Selma. First, we need to talk to Ali. I want you to call him and tell him where you are; tell him we have men ready to bring him here to you. Call him now. Here is your cell phone from your purse. Call him," the interrogator said.

Selma picked up her cell phone and dialed a number. No answer.

"Is this Ali?" The interrogator pulled out a photo he'd found in Selma's purse.

"Yes, it is," she said meekly. "Please don't hurt him."

"We will not if both of you cooperate. Now, why were you and your nephew following the Americans?" He leaned forward, inches from Selma's face.

"We were paid to do that. We needed money."

"Who paid you?"

"I don't know his name."

"Selma, you will go to prison if you lie to me. You don't expect me to believe you, do you? That a stranger gives you money to follow some people? Why would anybody do that?" he demanded.

"He told us, Ali and me, that he was with the police, some undercover, and that the people we were to follow were foreigners. They were dealing with drugs."

The interrogator looked at Natalie, almost asking if she believed the story.

The door to the interrogation room opened, and an assistant came in and whispered in the interrogator's ear. He nodded and motioned to Natalie to follow him. Natalie joined him, and they both left the room, leaving Selma there alone.

Outside, General Masoud was there with two other security men. "We have the cousin in custody. We are still looking for the nephew. We have been listening to what the old lady is saying. She may be lying. We don't know yet. Natalie, I'd like you to go back in there and continue with Selma. Ahmed, you have heard what Selma said; you go ahead with the cousin. I have a feeling he may be the mastermind. We have to get the facts very quickly before daybreak. Very urgent. I will be monitoring from here," Masoud said.

As the team of interrogators was ready to go back to questioning their suspect, a lieutenant rushed in with a note for the general. "The nephew was caught on a camera in an alley in Sharjah; they dispatched a team to the neighborhood. He was shown entering an old apartment building."

General Masoud went to the war room, with Natalie and the others close behind. On the screen, they watched three police cars arrive at the entry to the building. They were waiting for instructions. The general told them to wait. "Make sure all entrances are secure and wait for my instructions. I want the young nephew alive."

He told Natalie and the interpreter to go back to Selma. "Have her try again to call the nephew and ask him to surrender." They left immediately. Then he told Ahmed, "Go back to the cousin and tell him to do the same and ask the nephew to surrender."

The general called Mary. He gave her an update and expressed concern about the urgency to get Jennifer back before the press found out. Mary told him they were still waiting for a call from the kidnappers.

The general went back to the interrogation room and started watching Natalie and the old lady through the two-way mirror.

"Selma, I want you to call your nephew again. He is in Sharjah in a building that is surrounded by the police. He has to surrender; if he doesn't, he will be killed. Call him now; tell him to surrender to the police. They will bring him here. You must convince him; otherwise they will kill him." Natalie said, eyes focused on the old lady.

Selma gasped, started crying, and grabbed Natalie's hand, begging her not to hurt her nephew. Natalie gave Selma her cell phone and demanded she call her nephew. Selma picked up the phone and dialed the number. Ali answered immediately. He was sobbing.

"Ali, you are surrounded by the police. Please, my dear Ali, go outside and surrender. They promised they will not hurt you if you surrender. Go now; please go," Selma said, tears flowing over her wrinkled cheeks.

"They will kill me if I surrender. I know they will," Ali said.

"Ali, listen . . . they will kill you if you don't. Go now; you will be safe," Selma said.

———

Ali left his room quietly, took the elevator to the lobby, and slowly headed to the exit with his hands up in the air. He left the building, where police cars were waiting. He was immediately hand-cuffed, placed in one of the cars, and brought to the security head-quarters.

31

JEFF WAS IN his hotel room in San Francisco, anxiously waiting, when there was a knock on the door. It was Sam Kopitski, as expected. Sam went directly to the bar, mixed a scotch on the rocks, walked over to the sitting area, and sat down across from Jeff.

"Well, it looks like all hell has broken loose," Sam said. "Have you heard from Bill?"

"Not a word," Jeff replied.

"Neither has our friend. Do you think he has gone or is going to the authorities?" Sam asked.

"I think he will. He is panicked. He may feel his only way out is to cut a deal with our government," Jeff said.

"And say what? That his sophisticated server can become a lethal weapon or that the server has disappeared?" Sam was laying out the possible outcome.

"That may be the case, but right now he is frightened. I know Bill. He is suspecting us, doesn't trust us," Jeff said.

"Frankly, right now he is not what I am worried about. It is the box. Where is it? Who has it? How can this possibly happen?" Sam replied, worried. "Okay, Jeff. Let's assume that whoever has the box found out they could do nothing with it, so they kidnap the architect's wife to lure him in to unlock the mystery of the box, thinking he can."

"If they find out that the architect cannot, what will they do? Let them go and disappear? Kill him?" Jeff was not convinced.

"Wait a minute, the architect can activate the box. Bill gave him all the codes, but without the server, there is nothing he can do. We are back to: where is the server," Sam said.

"There is something wrong here. How can any team, no matter how sophisticated they are, pull off something like this unless they had inside help?" Sam added.

"I get your point. Think about it: what is the worst-case scenario for us?" Jeff asked.

"We get caught and go to jail."

"Okay. What has to happen for us to go to jail? What laws did we break?" Jeff was probing.

"The authorities find out about our plan to install a sophisticated server in a commercial building, approved by both our governments. However, if they find out that this same server can be converted into an offensive cyber weapon, that is against the law in both countries with severe consequences," Sam replied.

"Sam, let me say it again. If someone turns us in, like Bill or others, we say they are lying. Where is the proof?" Jeff demanded. "I know the box is gone, I know if they find it, it will not tell them anything without additional programming, and if Bill or others come forward, nobody will believe them without proof." Jeff was a bit agitated.

"What if more than one person comes forward? What if our partners here and in Dubai get nervous? What if many more know?" Sam was worried. Jeff knew this. He was too. He also knew it was too late to back out.

"Sam, I am concerned too, not as much as you perhaps. Here is the deal: we have no choice but to stay the course. It is too late to change anything. For now, stay calm and quiet, keep getting reports from the UAE, and take action when we need to."

"You are right. No turning back," Sam said.

"Just to be safe, I bought these two burner phones for you and me. Don't use any other phone when we talk; you never know," Jeff said.

"Yeah, you never know."

32

NATALIE WENT BACK to the room where Selma was after conferring with General Masoud about the nephew's surrender. The interpreter accompanied her.

Selma was still, quietly sobbing. Natalie sat down and offered her more tissues and a glass of water. She also had the interpreter bring a cup of tea for her.

Natalie asked Selma if she spoke English; she said yes but not very well. "Selma, now both your nephew and your cousin have been arrested. They are here in the building being questioned."

Selma immediately started sobbing and covered her face.

"It is very important that you answer my questions, if there is any hope of saving your nephew." Natalie placed her hand on Selma's arm. "Why were you following the Americans? Who told you to do that? I want the truth, Selma, the truth. It's the only thing that can help you and your nephew now."

Selma lifted her head up, wiped the tears, and looked directly at Natalie, who saw a woman who had suffered much, struggling to retain her dignity.

"My nephew and I were destitute. If it wasn't for my cousin, both of us may be dead now. He helped us; we stayed with him for a while. He helped us get jobs and was always there for us. He was like a father for my nephew." Selma stopped for a drink of water.

"Sometimes he would ask us to run some errands for him; he would pay us. Very helpful."

"What kind of errands?" Natalie asked.

"Small things like delivering packages to some people, picking up packages for him, and sometimes just following people and reporting back to him," Selma said.

"Who were the people? What was in the packages?" Natalie asked.

"I don't know. We were not allowed to open the packages. I don't know the people we delivered packages to and picked up packages from. There were several different people. All were in shops by the old souks."

"How about the people you were told to follow?"

"My nephew did all of that for them. I was only involved to help with the Americans," Selma replied.

"Who did your nephew tell you he was assigned to follow?"

"He told me they were all visitors, businesspeople or tourists from other countries, different countries. He usually followed them from the hotels."

"Okay, Selma. Now to the American and his wife. Who told you to follow them?" Natalie was looking straight into her eyes.

"It was my cousin."

"What were his orders exactly? I want all the details, from the very beginning."

"It was about a week ago. My cousin had a picture of this American he said would be arriving from Los Angeles. He told my nephew that he would be arriving within the next two or three days. He told my nephew what time each day they arrived, to wait for him, take pictures, and report back. He gave my nephew a special telephone to use. He gave me one too."

"What was your assignment? What did you do?" Natalie continued.

"My job was to be there with my nephew a couple of times so people don't become suspicious."

"Is that all you did?"

"No. I also took care of the small apartment they had rented under my name."

"You said 'they.' Who else was involved?"

"There was one other man. He was giving the orders. My cousin was afraid of him."

"Who was he?"

"I don't know his name. My cousin said he was with the police. My nephew and I were in two brief meetings with him."

"What did he look like?"

"He was tall and large. Scary. He dressed as an Emirati, but I thought he wasn't."

"What was the apartment for?"

"My cousin told us it was for a guest; they may or may not use it."

"Who was this guest? And why?" Natalie was feeling she may be getting close.

"We don't know. We were not told."

"What was your guess? What did your nephew think?"

"I thought it would be a woman, just the way I had to prepare the room," she said.

"Do you think it was planned for the American woman you and your nephew were following?"

"We didn't know. My nephew and I suspected it may be the American. We were very nervous and afraid," Selma said.

"Did you ask your cousin?"

"I did. He said not to worry. It was not my problem. I could tell he was also nervous."

"What were you supposed to do for this woman?"

"They told me because I was a nurse, my job was to keep the

guest calm and comfortable. Give her tranquilizers to keep her calm."

"Was kidnapping her part of the plan? Were you and your nephew part of the kidnapping?"

"No. It was supposed to be another team. Our job was to take care of the woman. That is all."

Natalie stood up and towered over Selma, glaring at her. "I told you the only way we can save you and your nephew is to tell the truth. Why are you lying to me?" she shouted.

Selma broke down, sobbing uncontrollably. "I swear on the graves of my husband and two children, I am telling the truth. They told us another team was involved."

"So, Selma, if you are telling the truth, why didn't they bring her to the apartment? Where did they take her?" Natalie said, angry.

Selma looked at Natalie, frightened and confused. "The kidnapping is scheduled for tomorrow. That is what they told us. Their plan was to bring the guest to the apartment tomorrow, scheduled for tomorrow. I swear to you." She broke down crying.

Natalie looked at Selma for a long time. She wasn't sure if she was telling the truth. If true, it definitely changed things. She handed her more tissue paper and walked out of the room.

General Masoud was outside the door, waiting. "I heard what she said. She is telling the truth. We are hearing the same thing from the nephew and the cousin. What I am focusing on is the leader who was giving orders. All three referred to him as being a policeman, a very large policeman. I have both our prisoners looking at photos of our officers who fit their description. We will know soon."

"That leaves us with more questions. Did the officer, whoever he may be, have another team deployed for the kidnapping without sharing with those three?" Natalie said.

"Or was this operation a completely separate group?" General Masoud said.

33

MARY AND RUSTY knocked on the hotel room door. Bill Sorenson opened it, and the two walked in. She did not wait for introductions or niceties.

"Mr. Sorenson, I am Mary Tobias from the CIA. You know why we are here. You have become a central figure in the kidnapping of Jennifer Sykes. Our mission is to bring her back safely and quickly. The longer this takes, the more volatile the situation. We need answers, and we need them now."

"Yes, Ms. Tobias, I know," he replied.

"Do you have any thoughts who the kidnappers may be?" Mary asked.

"Unfortunately, I don't," Bill said.

"Why would they kidnap Mrs. Sykes?"

"I am sure you know why. They are after her husband; they probably assumed they could not get to him, so they kidnapped her to bring him in."

"Mr. Sorenson, let me get right to the point. This whole thing is about CTC and your server. Whoever the kidnappers are, they must feel threatened by it. They are somehow assuming it is not just an advanced server but a weapon of some kind. We need to know everything about this server. Can it be converted into a cyber weapon? And where is it?" Mary demanded.

"It is a server; we call it the black box. It is part of the plan to install in the Al Bustan project for cybersecurity against cyberattacks," Bill said.

"Where is this box?" Mary asked. Bill hesitated. Mary pressed. "Where is the box, Mr. Sorenson?"

"I don't know."

"What do you mean you don't know? You'd better come clean, Mr. Sorenson. You could be in serious trouble if you don't." Mary grew impatient.

"The box was stolen. I checked earlier, and it was gone," Bill said.

"What the hell do you mean it was gone?" Mary screamed at him.

"Ms. Tobias, it is gone, but I had a duplicate of the black box made. I hid both in two different locations."

"Wait a minute. Why did you do that?" Mary demanded.

"To protect it from exactly what just happened."

"Okay. I will get back to that. So which box was stolen?" Mary asked.

"They are identical," Bill said.

"There has to be a difference. What are you hiding? What is the difference between the two?"

"They are identical. Both look the same and have the same components, with one major difference. To be operational, they both need to be programmed. They both function with enhanced cyber defense capabilities, as we have proposed."

"I get that, but what is the difference?" May said.

"One box has an added physical internal attachment that is essential, that enhances its capabilities; the other does not. Both have to be programmed; otherwise, they are useless. The other one does not have the attachment," Bill said.

"What is this attachment?" Mary asked.

"Highly classified," Bill said, almost whispering.

"Do you have clearance from the Department of Defense for this highly classified hardware?" Mary asked.

Bill did not answer. He stood up, took a couple of steps, and sat back down.

"Look, Mr. Sorenson, I need answers. I need them now. If we don't resolve the situation or if Mrs. Sykes is harmed and the story hits the press, I guarantee you will be the first that we go after. For starters, UAE internal security is ready to bring you in. They are waiting to hear from me. Now, for the last time, tell me everything you know about this black box. Who made it? What is its real purpose, and where is it?" Mary demanded.

"The box was produced by a joint effort of Sebastian Corporation and CTC and promoted by the two companies to military and commercial users. We have worked in collaboration with the Department of Defense. Because of the nature of this hardware, we need the DoD's approval for applications outside the US. The box is the data collector from an enormous number of sensors and microprocessors that feed it billions of pieces of data. The box is programmed to absorb, analyze, and act based upon the data received."

"How does that become a threat?" Mary said.

"It isn't, until we add the special attachment that enhances its capabilities further, enabling it to intercept and reverse cyberattacks," Bill said.

"Wait a minute. A black box with that kind of capability and highly classified, you need security clearance, which you don't have, do you?" Mary said.

"No, we don't. The enhancement was development by the two companies. They do not have approval yet for its use," Bill whispered.

"I need the names of who else is part of this. For now, how does the architect fit into all this? Why is he perceived to be so critical?" Mary asked.

"The architect is an expert in the placement of sensors and

microprocessors throughout a building for data collection. The programming of how to use that data is critical."

"If the architect is able to do that, why couldn't that also be performed by technical experts?" Mary asked.

"They can learn over time and through trial and error, physical experimentation. It takes time. Andy Sykes is one of maybe two or three people capable and experienced to make this work. He is unique in that he is both an experienced architect and a technology expert. Our mission is to have this advanced hardware available everywhere for enhanced cybersecurity," Bill said.

"So the bottom line is the kidnappers may have the box that is not the highly classified server. It does not have the attachment. What is stolen is the legitimate server that is planned for the project. An experienced programmer like Mr. Sykes is needed to make it all work, but without the box, he is useless. Do I have this right, Mr. Sorenson?" Mary said.

"Yes, you do."

"Okay, Mr. Sorenson. Where is the other box?" Mary demanded. Bill kept silent. "Mr. Sorenson, I suggest you think really hard about your situation before you answer me. Where is the box?"

"Before I tell you, I need immunity."

"You are in no position to demand anything. One phone call from me and you will land in prison so fast, you wouldn't know what hit you." Mary was angry.

"At the very least, I need a lawyer," he said.

"You get shit. You are in the UAE; the entire security system is mobilized to find a kidnapped American. With you as a key witness, if not a suspect, do you think anybody would give a shit what you demand? Now, for the last time, where is the box?" Mary was angry. Bill knew it.

"The box is hidden in an apartment building. I placed it there personally."

"How do you know it is still there? You already lost one," Mary said.

"Nobody but me knows where this is," Bill said.

Mary said nothing for a few minutes, absorbing what she heard. "Mr. Sorenson," she finally spoke, very calm and very determined. "I want you to answer three questions for me now. Your truthfulness and cooperation will determine what my recommendations will be regarding your future, so listen very carefully. One, who knew the location of the stolen box? Two, where is the other box? Three, who else is involved with you?" Mary stopped for a minute and then added, "Mr. Sorenson, don't play games. We know what is going on. This whole thing stinks. For your sake, and for the last time, you'd better answer all my questions."

Bill Sorenson, senior executive of CTC, sat upright, quietly staring at nothing but with a calm recognition and maybe relief that this was finally coming to an end. He thought about his wife and children, and Mary could almost see the tears swelling in his eyes.

"Okay, Ms. Tobias, I have already told you all about the box and its capabilities. The second box is experimental for this scale. If we are successful, it would be a major breakthrough for our company. We can promote and sell it to both public and private entities. We had to keep it secret, primarily because we may not receive approval from our government. We took the risk," Bill said.

"Mr. Sorenson, you are not telling me everything. For now, we are going to locate and retrieve the box. You show us where it is."

34

JENNIFER LOOKED AROUND the sparse, barely lit room. She continued pacing, waiting for someone, anyone, to show up. She was worried about Andy; she knew how strong he was, mentally and emotionally, but she also knew what Andy was thinking. It was all about finding a way to free her, and that meant giving himself up for her. So far, none of her kidnappers had talked to her. It had to be soon. She continued pacing; it was her way to calm down and think clearly, an old habit since she was young.

She knew they wanted Andy. They wanted a trade. She also knew that Andy would accept with conditions. She was expecting movement, surprised that nothing had happened so far.

The door opened, and the young woman who called herself Amina walked in with a tray of snacks. She set it down and asked Jennifer if there was anything she needed.

"I want to know how much longer I have to stay as your prisoner," she said.

"Very soon. Contact with your husband is being planned as we speak," Amina said.

"Do I get a chance to talk to him? He is very worried."

"Yes, you will. They will be coming here soon. You will get a chance to talk to him."

As Amina finished speaking, the door opened. There was a man fully dressed in black with a mask that covered his face except for his eyes. "Hello, Mrs. Sykes. Our apologies for this inconvenience. I hope you have been treated well," he said.

Interesting accent, Jennifer thought. "I have been treated well for being a prisoner. When are you going to release me? You know I have nothing of value," Jennifer said, probing.

"Mrs. Sykes, we are going to call your husband now. We have an encrypted and totally safe, untraceable cell phone. We have your husband's number. We want you to tell him that you are safe and have been treated well. That should not be a problem for you. By now, you know any other message of any kind would not help you or your husband. Understood?" he said.

"Yes. Understood," Jennifer replied.

He pulled out a cell phone and punched in the numbers. After three rings, Andy answered. "Hello?"

"Hello, Mr. Sykes. We have your wife. We wanted to let you know she is well. You can ask her yourself. Before you do, I want you to understand that if you want to see your wife again, ever again, you will do exactly what we tell you. Here she is," the kidnapper said and handed the cell phone to Jennifer.

"Andy, it's me. Please don't worry, sweetheart. I am okay, considering. I love you. We will be together soon. I know we will," Jennifer said.

Before Andy could respond, the kidnapper grabbed the cell phone from Jennifer. "Now you know she is fine. We are going to—"

"No, no way. I need to talk to my wife before I listen to any of your threats," Andy shouted.

"Okay. You have one minute." The kidnapper passed the phone to Jennifer.

"Darling, I love you. I promise you we will be together soon, free from all this. Are you sure they are treating you well?" Andy was trying not to break down, but Jenn was always the strong one.

"I am okay, really. Just see what it is they want and get me out of here. I love you."

The masked man took the phone away from her. "Mr. Sykes, your wife is fine. She will not be harmed as long as you work with us. Understood?" the man said.

"Where is my wife? I want to talk to her more," Andy screamed at him.

"She is fine. Now it is just you and me. I am sure you know what we want," the man said.

"No, I don't. I really don't. What do you want?"

"Mr. Sykes, we have the box."

That hit Andy like a bolt of lightning. He froze. "What box? I don't know anything about a box."

"Mr. Sykes, do not play games with us. We need you to make it operational, program it," he demanded.

"I am telling you the truth. I have never seen this box." Andy decided to be honest with this guy. "I know it is part of the cybersecurity system we plan to design for the project. We are way too early for any implementation. We don't even have a signed contract."

"We know that, Mr. Sykes. We also are determined that this system does not get in place. It is a lethal offensive cyber weapon that is of significant threat to us."

"Who are you?" Andy had to ask.

"That doesn't matter, Mr. Sykes. You will know in time."

"What do you want from me? I honestly and truly have never seen this box and don't know how it works."

"That is okay, Mr. Sykes. You know much more than you think you know. More importantly, what you may not know, we do. In one hour, we will call you back and tell you where to go. We will direct you to Jennifer. She will be released immediately once you arrive. You will be with us for a maximum of twenty-four hours, ample time to understand the workings of the box. If in one hour, you do not do what we are asking of you, you will not see your wife again. One hour, Mr. Sykes." He hung up.

—

Andy stood up, pacing, not sure what to do. He was deep in thought. *This is crazy. What the hell are these people thinking? Who told them all this about me? How did they get the box? What do I do?*

Andy heard a knock at the hotel room door. Bob went to open it, and Mary walked in with Rusty and Bill Sorenson.

35

MARY LOOKED AT Bob and Andy and saw the anxiety on their faces. "What is going on? Did you get the call?" she asked.

"Yes," Bob said. "Andy just hung up with the kidnapper."

Andy told Mary about the conversation, that he let him talk to Jennifer and that she seemed to be okay. "He told me they have the box," Andy said.

Mary gasped. "Andy, Bill told me that the box was stolen a few days ago. Only one other person besides Mr. Sorenson knew where the box was."

"Who? Who knew?" Andy was angry.

"You will know soon. That is not important now. The box they stole is not programmed, but they assume you can activate it," Mary said.

"Jesus. Those guys don't know that. They think I can activate it, but I can't. I have not seen it. What if they find out? Oh, my God, Jennifer is in real danger. They may kill her and destroy the evidence. We can't let that happen. They can't find out," Andy said. "We have one hour. One hour to figure this out. What are we going to do?"

"They don't need to know that you have not had access to the server. You can activate because you know the codes." Bill added.

"What if it doesn't work, I miss a number, or it has not been tested? How does that help Jennifer?" Andy demanded.

"Remember Andy, the server self destructs, if not programmed precisely or any attempt to physically access it," Bill said.

"Andy, we have to think this through. They will be calling in less than an hour. They want you as a swap for Jennifer. We have to buy time somehow. We need time to have the right plan in place that brings Jennifer back safely and gets you out safely also," Mary said.

"We have to find out where they will be taking you. We have to have guarantees that Jennifer is released. We cannot have any tracking devices on you. They will screen you early on, before you get to the final destination. We have to find an alternative way of finding out where you are held," Mary said.

"General Masoud's team, as well as our people, will be on standby throughout the city to move in quickly. Andy, there is no getting around this: you will be at high risk. We may not get to you in time. What you have to do is buy time. Work on the box; find reasons why it is taking so long." Mary stopped for a moment.

"How do I stall them? They were persistent on the timing," Andy said, not sure how this was going to end. "What kind of assurance can I get that Jennifer is okay and will be released?"

"Andy, here is what you should do. When they call, you insist that Jennifer be released first. They will refuse. Then you demand that during your journey to them via instructions you received, they bring Jennifer to a public place that you chose. You tell them you know your wife has to be part of the plan. The situation is very fluid; we have to adjust as events dictate," Mary said, laying out the plan.

"In the meantime, we have to figure out a way to locate you."

"Well, here is the problem. They expect me to start working on the box, which I have never seen and don't know how it works. I have, I think, the instructions, the codes memorized, but they were never tested. They apparently have technical experts who I am sure are much more knowledgeable than I and can see right through my ignorance." He was not at all confident.

"Andy, Mary," Bill Sorenson jumped in. "Let me go right now and retrieve the second box. It will take me about half an hour to forty minutes. I can show you the box, walk you through it. I don't know all its capabilities but enough to give you a fighting chance. If you give yourself more time, it would be helpful."

"I like it. Andy, what do you think?" Mary said.

"Yes, anything right now would help."

"Rusty, go with Bill. You drive. Try to make it back as fast as you can. I don't want to alert local security right now. We need the box back in our possession," Mary said.

Bill and Rusty left.

"Andy, are you okay? This is a huge burden on you. You must be terribly worried about Jennifer. We will do whatever it takes to get her back safely. You are going to be doing all the heavy lifting. Stay calm. Don't react to their provocation," Mary said.

Bob came over and sat beside Andy, putting his arm around him. "Okay, buddy. I know you, and I love you and Jenn. I know how difficult this is. I also know how smart you are. If anybody can make this work, you can."

Andy stood up, looked outside for a long time, then turned around.

"Bob, you are right. There is no way I am going to let them hurt her. They may be a bunch of thugs, but I am smarter. I will get her back, Bob. I will," Andy said as he slowly lifted his fist in the air.

36

THE INTERROGATION ROOM where Yahia Hamzi, Selma's cousin, was being questioned was stark. There was a table with Yahia sitting on one side and two interrogators on the other. A third was standing directly behind Yahia, a computer screen placed in front of him. General Masoud was watching through the two-way glass mirror.

Yahia was shaking and in tears. He was handcuffed to his chair.

"Look at the screen; you will see the images of our officers who match the description you gave us. Take your time, watch carefully, and let us know if you find the officer you claim hired you," the lead interrogator said. As he clicked the screen on, images of four men appeared.

Yahia looked closely, still shaking, sweat dripping from his forehead. He shook his head and said no to the four. The screen changed with images of four more men. Yahia shook his head again. In each case, the interrogator instructed Yahia to take his time and make sure none of the images was that of the leader, supposedly a police officer.

Yahia began to cry, begging the interrogators for forgiveness, insisting he was not a party to any kidnapping. The interrogators ignored him and continued to show images of the police officers until they exhausted the list. The lead interrogator stood up and walked out of the room.

General Masoud, who was watching, nodded to the captain standing beside him. The captain instructed the interrogator to go ahead and show the next group, the special security unit.

Yahia was focused on the new images that the interrogator was showing him. He was taking his time as he scrutinized each face carefully. There were no matches—until the sixth screen. "There he is, the leader who was giving the orders. That is him—that is Khalil. That is the man who told us he was an officer," Yahia shouted. He was animated but could not move because of the handcuffs.

"Did you say Khalil? Khalil what?" the interrogator asked.

"Just Khalil; that is what he said his name was, just Khalil," Yahia said.

The interrogator downloaded the photo and the associated information from the computer and rushed out. He told General Masoud, "The man identified by Yahia is Saleem Abdul Rahman, a ten-year member of the elite unit." The general recognized him and ordered the captain to find him and bring him there.

The captain picked up his cell and called the security unit leader, Saleem's boss. A minute later, he reported back to the general. "General, he didn't report to work today; he told his leader he had to take his son to the hospital for an emergency and promised to come to work soon. He has not arrived yet."

"Find him. Get the word out; do not let him leave the country," the general ordered.

The captain rushed out, and the general went back to the war room. He looked at the screens that his men were monitoring but did not notice anything unusual.

He went back to the interrogation rooms to watch the three ongoing interrogations. His cell phone buzzed; it was the captain. "General, Officer Saleem Abdul Rahman is not at his home; neither is any members of his family. None of his children have attended school today."

"He is on the run," the general said. "Check all borders, airports, and train stations. Alert all our officers and police. Activate our war room search. I want him. Now go."

37

A NDY WAS PACING; he could not sit still, Mary stood up and started pacing with him. They were anxiously waiting, rehearsing, and trying to predict what the kidnappers' requirements might be, when her cell phone buzzed. It was Natalie.

"Mary, General Masoud's men have located and arrested the apparent leader of the crew. He is the cousin's boss, recruiter, or whatever he is. He is in charge. The cousin identified him from photos. Apparently, he was planning to leave Dubai with his family when he was apprehended. They are questioning him right now. The way it is going, it shouldn't be very long. I wanted to give you a heads up before I go back to watch and listen."

"Do you still believe the woman and her nephew were helping the police? You believe them?" Mary asked.

"I don't know yet. I will get back to you."

———

Natalie hung up and went back to the two-way mirror, watching the new prisoner. He was one of General Masoud's special unit security men. He was tall and muscular, typical of the handpicked and well-trained men whom the general had insisted upon. It was a prerequisite for joining his force.

He was Egyptian, not unusual for the security and police force. They were disciplined and loyal. But to have one of his men betray the security force was very disturbing. For General Masoud, it was personal.

Whatever motivated this prisoner to betray his employer, knowing the severity of the punishment, had to be significant. A large reward.

General Masoud was part of the core leadership dedicated to transforming Dubai into one of the safest and most secure large cities in the entire Middle East, if not globally. They developed and trained a police force of around seventeen thousand members and created a police academy that, by any standards, was one of the best in training officers not only about police work but also the law, community policing, psychology, and the best use of technology. They were committed to having cameras in place on every street corner and building in the city, along with police kiosks throughout the city, equipped with the latest application of AI that allows citizens immediate and easy access to the police.

This was personal. This was betrayal. This was an insult.

General Masoud was standing next to Natalie, watching and listening intently and calmly, without showing any outward emotion.

"Saleem, you know you will be severely punished for your crime. There is no forgiveness. You have betrayed all of us and this country that has been very generous to you and your family," the interrogator started. "The three who have been taking your orders have told us everything. Now you will tell us everything. You tell us about your plans, the kidnapping, other people involved. Who is directing you, who is paying you? You will tell me everything. You do not deserve any mercy, but your wife and four children do. Do you understand what I am telling you?"

"Yes," Saleem said with his head down, his face covered with bruises.

"Alright. Where is she? Mrs. Sykes, the American woman you kidnapped?"

"I don't know anything about any kidnapping," Saleem said.

"Stop. Right now," The interrogator shouted. "Yesterday, early afternoon, you and a team using three vehicles managed to abduct the American. You knew the route and the place where the American was going. You and your team kidnapped her. Now, again, where is she?"

"I swear by my four children, I swear that God strike me dead if I am lying. I had nothing to do with any kidnapping."

"Enough," the interrogator said as he slapped Saleem, who was handcuffed. "I warned you not to lie to me. Your entire family is in great danger of being accused as your accomplices if you lie to me."

"I swear to God I have not been involved with this kidnapping," Saleem said.

"You directed your team to follow the woman who was kidnapped. You lied to them about the Americans being drug dealers. You told your team to keep an apartment you rented ready for the woman you were planning to kidnap. You even told them to be ready for instructions. Do you deny any of this?"

"Sir, I am sorry. I am so sorry." Saleem was sobbing. "I was taking orders. I was paid a lot of money to follow the Americans. They told me there will be a kidnapping. They told me the Americans stole millions of dollars' worth of drugs from them. They wanted it back. They told me they will hold the woman for a couple of hours and release her."

"How much did they pay you?"

"They paid me twenty thousand dollars and promised another twenty thousand when the whole thing was over. He told me nobody would get hurt." With his head down, Saleem was sobbing so hard that the interrogator pushed the Kleenex box to him.

"Stop crying. You are an embarrassment. Who gave you the money? How many people were there?"

"There was always just one man."

"Who is he? What is his name?"

"He called himself Nick. He was a foreigner. That is all I know about him."

"Where did you meet?"

"We always met early in the morning in a coffee shop on Sheikh Zayed Road. He knew my shift. Always half an hour before my shift. Meetings were always less than ten minutes."

"How often did you meet?"

"We met every day." Saleem heaved a sigh but had stopped crying.

"Where does this Nick live?"

"I don't know."

"Describe him."

"He is tall and large like me. He has very dark curly hair and a mustache. Always wears blue jeans and a dark shirt."

"What country is he from?"

"I don't know that, but he is definitely European."

"How about an accent? British, Irish, French, Italian? Could you tell from your experience as a policeman?"

"He was none of those nationalities. He may be Eastern European. Could be Greek or Turkish too."

"Iranian?"

"I don't think so. I know many Iranians here. It was not their accent."

"When was the last time you talked to him?"

"Yesterday morning."

"What was discussed?"

"He was very brief. He said to be ready to go ahead with the plan within a day."

"That means today, right?"

"Yes."

"Now, Saleem, you listen to me very carefully. Yesterday, early afternoon, Mrs. Sykes, the American, was abducted. That morning, you say he met with you and told you to be ready for the next day. Now I want you to think very hard. If what you tell us is true, why do you think he was using you? Assuming that he and his team did the kidnapping, what was your use?"

Saleem was quiet. He didn't say anything. He was thinking. He quit sobbing. "Please, sir, give me a moment. Let me think back on all that happened." He finally straightened up and looked directly at the interrogator.

"He did not use me to shift the blame on me. He is too smart for that. He also knew how good our security system is, that sooner or later, more likely sooner, he would be caught.

"The only reason he used us was first to follow the Americans. Their true purpose with us was not about blaming us but to give them the time. They knew the attention, your attention, was to find us. They needed that small amount of time to do what they have planned. We were the diversion," Saleem said, a policeman again.

"Sir, in my opinion, whatever they are planning, it will happen very soon. Sir, I have done wrong. I have betrayed you. You will punish me, I know that, and I deserve the punishment. Please, let me help. Let me be part of the team looking for them. You know I cannot and will not escape."

The interrogator looked at the two-way mirror. Before he could signal, the door opened, and General Masoud entered. He looked straight at Saleem and told him to stand up. Saleem did. The general reeled back and, with all his force, slapped Saleem. Saleem fell back.

The general looked at Saleem, straightening his uniform. "I will deal with your punishment later. Now I need you. What do you think they are planning to do and how soon?"

"Sheikh Masoud, they are after the husband, but we knew he was well guarded. They kidnapped her to get him. They came referring to the 'package.' I'm not sure what exactly the package was; they told me it was some kind of weapon. They gave me the impression they needed the architect to open it, some secret code," Saleem said.

"What were they planning to do with it?" General Masoud asked.

"They implied they needed to give it to some third party. It was important to them to get this done in twenty-four hours," Saleem said.

General Masoud was quiet, staring at Saleem. Then he said, "I want you to go and work with my team to identify and get the man you have been working with. One more thing: how did you find out the route the architect's wife was taking? Nobody knew ahead of time. Who shared that with you?"

"Your Excellency, nobody told me anything about this route. I don't know anything about it," Saleem said.

The general looked at Saleem for a long time and then left the room. He picked up his cell phone and called Mary to tell her they needed to meet.

38

BILL SORENSON GAVE Rusty the address and the directions for how to get there. They arrived at a residential high-rise building. They parked the car in the garage below and headed to the elevators. Bill pressed the twenty-sixth floor.

There were four apartments on each floor. Bill went directly to apartment 2603 and pulled out his key to unlock the door. However, the door was already unlocked.

Bill looked at Rusty. Rusty pulled Bill back, took out his gun, and quietly stepped into the room. The place was completely torn apart. Furniture strewn all over the place, cushions torn, and holes in all the walls with sheet rock removed. It was a total disaster.

Rusty came to a complete stop when he saw the body. It was a man, face down. He wasn't sure if he was alive or dead. He approached the body and saw dried blood on the back of his head. He felt his pulse; the man was still alive.

Bill walked in and saw the body. "Oh, my God. Oh, my God." That was all he could say.

"Who is he? Do you know him?" Rusty asked.

"Yes. Yes, I do. This is Tyler, Tyler Grant, the architect that STR just hired."

"Where is the box? Did they take the box?"

"I can't believe this. This is terrible, just terrible," Bill said, very emotional.

"Bill, get a hold of yourself. Where is the box? Did they take it?" Rusty demanded.

"No, I don't think so. Come with me. We need an ambulance. We need to get him to the hospital," Bill said.

Rusty picked up his phone and dialed Mary. He explained what happened. "I'll call Natalie to get a team to the apartment ASAP. In the meantime, find the box and bring it back to the hotel," she demanded.

Bill went to the master bathroom, which was torn up just like the bedroom. The walls in the bathroom were also torn apart. The cover of the electric panel was removed. Bill stepped over all the debris and walked directly to the electrical panel. He leaned in, looking up. The panel was recessed around three inches.

He reached up to the opening above the electric panel and started searching with his fingers until he found the small latch and pulled it. The panel started opening very slowly. It opened enough for him to reach behind it, find the second latch, and pull. The solid steel panel below the electrical panel opened.

There was nothing in there; the space was empty: no black box or anything else. Whoever took it closed the panel behind them.

Bill screamed. He kept pushing and searching, hoping it was there. It wasn't. Rusty reached in to help search for the box. No luck. Bill kept staring at the empty space, not sure what to do. He was in total panic mode and kept repeating, "This can't be . . . this can't be."

"I need to call Mary. Let her know. We'd better get out of here and head back. This definitely complicates everything. We will leave the door unlocked for our team to take care of Tyler," Rusty said.

They left the apartment. Rusty closed the door and left it unlocked. They headed downstairs to the car. Rusty called Mary and told her they were on their way. He also told her about the disappearance of the box.

"I will contact General Masoud and let him know what happened after the CIA team gets there and takes care of Tyler," she said. Rusty gave her the address and the apartment number.

Bill and Rusty headed back to the hotel. It was almost the time when the kidnappers said they would call back. They were not sure how this was going to play out.

"If the kidnappers were the ones who ransacked the apartment, they know about the box—maybe both boxes. Who else was looking for the box and may have attacked Tyler? What was Tyler doing there in the first place? This changes everything," Mary said to Rusty and Bill when she walked up to the car.

"It sure does, Mary; it sure does," Rusty said.

39

MARY DID NOT tell Andy about Tyler. She took Bob aside and told him that Tyler was Bill Sorenson's inside man. "Something must have gone wrong. Tyler may have double-crossed Bill as well," she added.

Mary and Bob came back to the sitting area. "Andy, the apartment where Bill had the box hidden was completely ransacked when he and Rusty arrived. Unfortunately, whoever demolished the place found and took the second box. Now we have both stolen," Mary said. "Bill and Rusty are on their way up. They should be here any moment. We don't know who was searching for the box and how they knew where to look for it. If this was the kidnappers, the plan changes completely. They would know the box they have may be different. That will harden their position now that they may have both. You have to be prepared to adjust to this change. What we need now, more than anything, is time."

Bill and Rusty walked in, and Bill immediately sat down. They all stared at him, a totally exhausted man, his fear and panic resonating from his sweating forehead.

Andy immediately stood up and walked toward Bill, glaring at him. "This is all your fault, you son of a bitch. You lied to us; you betrayed us. If anything happens to Jennifer, I swear I . . . " Andy did not finish his sentence.

He turned to face Mary. "Now what do we do? We are screwed. They will never let Jennifer go," Andy said.

"We don't know, Andy. We just don't know what they have. We just have to wait and see," Mary said.

"Bill, who else knew where this box was hidden?" Bob asked.

"No one, I swear. Someone must have followed me," Bill said.

"You have to have the codes to be able to activate it, correct? So the box is useless without that," Bob said.

"Yes."

"Do the kidnappers know this?"

"I am sure they do," Bill answered.

"If they know that, they have to know this is a highly classified piece of equipment. They must think that I have the code numbers," Andy said.

"I agree. They must believe you have the code for one or both boxes," Mary said.

"Andy has the code, so they believe they can use Jennifer to get him to activate the server," Bill said, getting engaged.

"Look, Andy, all of you, I know what I have done; you can deal with me later. For now, we have a mission: get Jennifer back, protect Andy, and retrieve the boxes, in that order. You must trust me." Bill stood up and looked at the angry faces, searching for redemption, if not forgiveness.

"Dammit, Bill, you lied to us; you should have had all these security details worked out before we started. You gave me the code to activate that I had to memorize, but I have not seen or tested this server. What if it doesn't work?" Andy shouted.

"Bob, Andy, here's the deal. We have one shot at this. We don't know if they have one or both boxes. It doesn't matter; they need Andy to activate, period. Andy must stall for time as long as he can. At the end, he should try to activate it and hope it works," Bill said.

"Bill is right, Andy. If they press you, you try to activate it; if it does not work, you make excuses, such as the computer they provided you is inadequate. Stall, delay, do what you have to until we find you," Mary said.

"Okay. I hope I can remember the code. I will bring my computer; hopefully it can talk to this box." Andy went to the bedroom and brought out his PC.

"No, Andy, that is too risky. They will confiscate it and have access to whatever is in it," Mary said.

Andy looked to Bill in exasperation and panic. Before he could say anything, his cell phone rang. They all stopped in attention. Andy picked up his phone and took a deep breath. "Hello," he said.

"Hello, Mr. Sykes. It is time. You follow our instructions precisely as we tell you, and Mrs. Sykes will be returned to you unharmed. You have our word."

"I need to talk to my wife," Andy said.

"Not yet. I assure you she is fine. You will talk to her once you start following our orders."

"How do I know she is okay?"

"She is. You have no choice but to take my word for it."

"Please, you are making a serious mistake. I don't know anything about whatever you have and whatever you think I can do. Just let my wife go."

"Mr. Sykes, we don't have much time. You do what we tell you. If you don't, you will never see your wife again. Is that clear? If you refuse, you will not hear from me again. No more games. Do you understand what I am telling you?"

Andy looked at the others in the room, pleading for help. Mary motioned to him to accept. He knew there was no other option. "Alright. What do you want me to do?"

"Leave the hotel right now; take a taxi to the Dubai Fountain by Burj Khalifa. Have your cell phone with you. I will call you there. Mr. Sykes, no tracking devices, no electronic nonsense; please come alone." He hung up.

"Okay, Andy, they are going to have you go through the hoops.

These guys are pros. Way before the final destination, they will have somebody approach you. You will be checked for any devices. We can't take that risk. Somewhere during the trip, you demand no further running around until you talk to Jennifer and she is released. It is not obvious if they know about the second black box," Mary said.

Walking over to him, she said, "Andy, we can track you through your cell phone. Give it to me. I will configure it. I will also give you this small phone that looks like a hearing aid; you will communicate with me. When they search you, it would probably be discovered. So just before that, I want you to swallow it. Don't worry; it will not harm you. It will continue to give us the signals from inside your stomach. I will be with you the whole way. We have ways to keep an eye on you."

"Okay, I'd better get started. I will stay in touch until I can't. I assume you will have Dubai security notified. Whatever you do, you can't give them an excuse to hurt Jennifer."

They all stood up, watching Andy go toward the door. He suddenly turned around. "Did you notice his English was quite good? A definite Eastern European accent, sounded Ukrainian." Then he left the room.

Mary went to the bedroom and called Tim Patterson. He picked up immediately. "Mary, what is happening? I have not heard from you."

"Tim, listen, I don't have time to give you details. I will later. The kidnappers contacted Andy; he is following their instructions. The objective here is a swap, him for his wife," Mary said.

"Wait a minute, Mary, are you sure about this? The architect is way too valuable. We cannot afford to lose him."

"That is not our choice; it is his," Mary said.

40

MAJOR GARFIELD WALKED in the room, joining Mary and her team. She requested that he meet them after sharing with him the latest news. She wanted him to help in interrogating Bill and Tyler in the consulate.

Bill, Rusty, and Bob were in the room with Mary, who was on her cell phone. She motioned for Chuck to join them. "That was General Masoud," she said, hanging up. "He wants me to join him in his war room, monitoring Andy's movements."

Just then, two of the local CIA agents walked in with Tyler with a bandage wrapped around his head. Bob did not stand up to greet Tyler, who avoided looking at him.

"Tyler, Bill, you will go back to the consulate with Major Garfield and Rusty, where you will surrender your passports. You are not allowed to leave the consulate. There, you will be questioned. You will tell them everything. You both have broken both US and UAE laws. The legal system will deal with you. Many questions need to be answered, but for now, our total focus is to protect Andy and bring Jennifer back unharmed. You two will help," Mary said. "Rusty, you and one of your team go with Major Garfield and help get Bill and Tyler to the consulate. Stay there and help Chuck. You will hear back from me. Go now."

When they turned to leave, she said, "Bob, you come with me to General Masoud's headquarters. I need you to stay close as we monitor what's going on with Andy. Okay, everybody, let's go. Keep your cell phones handy."

41

MARY AND BOB left for General Masoud's headquarters; the rest left for the consulate. On the way, Mary called Natalie, who picked up immediately. She briefed Natalie and let her know she was on her way.

Natalie told her, "We've made some progress toward identifying the kidnappers. I'll give you the details once you arrive."

When they got there, the huge war room was lit up, each screen monitored by trained security specialists. The screens showed activities throughout the city—in the streets, public spaces, public buildings, garages, and major building entrances. An impressive use of the latest technology.

General Masoud, his senior officers, and Natalie were monitoring Andy's location and movements. "Andy has just arrived at the Dubai Fountain. We are looking at the cameras by the fountain. He is sitting on a bench," Natalie said.

Mary said, "I'll call him." Andy answered through his earphones. "Hi, Andy, this is Mary. How are you holding up?"

"So far, nothing. I am anxious, worried about Jennifer, but I'm okay."

"Andy, we are monitoring your movements. The security forces are mobilized and instructed to help find Jennifer and protect both of you. We are watching you on the screen," Mary said.

"I know. That's comforting," Andy said.

"Good. Hang in there." She hung up and turned toward the general. "Okay, General, Natalie said you made some progress on the identity of the kidnappers."

"The person who provided the routine information to the kidnappers was one of my security men. He will be dealt with when this is over. However, he has been very helpful. We questioned the owner and the staff of the coffee shop where the meetings with the kidnapper took place. They seem to think he was Russian or Ukrainian, definitely Slavic. The café did not have any internal cameras, so we looked at the closest ones. Based on the information from the staff, we developed a credible description of the man and found a match on one of the street cameras a block away from the café. It was on the morning of the kidnapping, the last time our officer met him," the general said.

"That is good progress, Masoud," Mary said.

"We could not see his face very clearly, but he was dressed exactly as the officer described: jeans, dark shirt, cowboy boots, and with a mustache. We checked our data base, starting with Russians and Ukrainians. Nothing so far. We are still searching."

"How about other nationalities, Eastern European or others?"

"We are looking at anyone who might match."

"How about cameras throughout the city, different times, different places?" Mary asked.

"We are doing that too," he said.

Onscreen, they heard Andy's cell phone buzz and watched him pick it up.

"Mr. Sykes, please walk into Dubai Mall and go to the second floor. As you enter, you will see a directory. Find a restaurant called La Mama. It is less than fifty yards on your left. Go there, order an espresso, and wait." He hung up.

Andy got up and started walking to the mall. "Did you hear all that?" he asked; the earpiece picked it up.

"Yes, Andy, we did. We are with you," Mary said. She looked at the general.

"I have our men around there. They will be alerted," General Masoud said.

"Why the crowded mall?" Mary asked.

"It is a smart move. We will find out," he answered.

The cameras were already showing the activities inside the mall. One camera zeroed in on the restaurant's sign, written in large letters. Other cameras inside the mall were tracking all other activities. Andy entered the mall and went straight to the directory.

They watched Andy walk toward the restaurant. The mall was crowded. All kinds of people—Europeans, Asians, Emiratis—were walking and shopping, a typical morning. They watched Andy arrive at the restaurant and get seated. He ordered an espresso.

Mary was watching for any unusual movement close to where Andy was sitting. Nothing out of the ordinary. Andy ordered a second espresso. It had been at least fifteen minutes of waiting.

A young woman appeared, European, approaching the restaurant. Andy was sitting in their outside seating area. The woman walked straight to Andy and sat down at his table. Andy was not sure what to do. He looked at her. She was in her twenties, very attractive, and dressed well.

"May I help you?" Andy said.

"Hello, Mr. Sykes. You are Andy Sykes, right?" she said.

"Yes, I am."

"I have a message for you, Mr. Sykes."

"A message from whom? You didn't tell me your name."

"How rude of me. Terribly sorry. My name is Molly." She extended her hand to shake his.

"What is the message?" Andy asked.

"The message is from your wife."

Andy was quiet. *Is this real? What are they up to?* "What is the message?" he asked.

"The message is she loves you very much and not to wait for her. She will be late."

"Was that all?"

"Oh, she said to tell you to be careful."

"Did she give you the message herself?"

"No. A friend of hers did."

"Who was this friend?"

"A young woman I never met before. She gave me one hundred dollars to deliver it. She told me you would understand."

Andy stood up, totally frustrated.

"I am sorry, Mr. Sykes. Did I say something wrong? I was just delivering a message. Terribly sorry." She stood up to leave.

Out of nowhere, two men came by, showed her their police badges, grabbed her by the arm, and asked her to go with them.

"Mary, they are playing with me." Andy was stressed.

"Andy, listen . . . yes, they are. They want to weaken you, play with your emotions. They will be contacting you very soon."

Andy's cell phone rang, and he answered. "Mr. Sykes, as we thought, you have security people all around you. We told you to come alone. You haven't. For the rest of your trip, you get the word to the people watching you to back off. In five minutes, an Emirati gentleman will come to you and ask you to follow him. You follow him. And by the way, he doesn't know anything either. Tell your security people to back off. Don't waste time." He hung up.

General Masoud sent word to his people to stay back. "He will play their game. These guys are pros," he told Mary.

Natalie was standing next to them. She was watching the screen very intently and listening to the conversations on loudspeaker.

"Masoud, now we think the kidnappers may be Russians, based on what your officer told you and verified by the cameras. Is that right?" Mary said.

"Russian intelligence? That doesn't make sense. Why would they take such a huge risk and alienate us? We have good relations," the general said, not convinced.

"I agree, General," Mary said.

"But the kidnappers appear to be Russians," Natalie said. "Let's assume for the moment they are. Look at the options: Russian security, surrogates hired by the Russian government or by another government, or Russian mafia driven by money."

"The only two plausible options are the Russian mafia on their own for the money or Russians hired by somebody powerful, which means a government, corporation, or wealthy individuals," the general said.

The three security heavyweights looked at each other, each feeling confidence they were on the right track.

"You know what this means. No matter who is behind this, the execution is the Russian mafia," Mary said.

42

"**A**NDY, LISTEN. WE think the people may be Russian mafia. That may change things a bit. The only thing they care about is money. They must be after the box so they can sell it. They must think it would be extremely valuable for some government to buy it from them," Mary said, as Andy was waiting at La Mama for the kidnappers' next move.

"We believe you need to turn the tables on them. Let them know you can make the box operational, but it will take time. You have to insist that Jennifer be released first. Any other way, you will lose your leverage."

Andy listened to Mary. "Makes sense. At the end of the day, it is up to me. I have to get Jennifer out. It has to be my way," he said.

An Emirati man was walking toward Andy and stopped in front of him. "Mr. Sykes, come with me please," he said.

Andy got up and followed him, as per instructions. They went down the elevator to the garage. He had a white Toyota SUV and asked Andy to get in the passenger seat, which he did.

They left the garage. Andy wasn't sure where they were going. "Where are we going?" he asked the driver.

"They will let me know soon."

The driver's phone buzzed. He picked it up, but Andy couldn't hear what was said. The driver kept nodding. Then he hung up but didn't say anything to Andy.

Andy's phone buzzed. It was the kidnapper. "Mr. Sykes, in five minutes, the driver will drop you off in front of a building. You go inside and take the elevator to the twenty-third floor, room 2308. The door will be unlocked. You just walk in and wait." He hung up before Andy could say anything.

The car arrived at the building. The driver did not say a word, just waited for Andy to get out of the car.

Before going inside the building, Andy called Mary. "Did you hear all that?"

"Yes, we did. We know where you are. We are checking the address to see who owns the unit."

Andy went inside the building, directly to the elevators. He pushed the button, and the elevator door opened on the twenty-third floor. Andy stepped out, his heart beating fast. Not knowing what to expect, he found number 2308 written in bronze on a solid door. He turned the handle; it was unlocked. Andy walked in. It was a nicely furnished two-bedroom apartment. Nothing out of place, no clutter, very clean.

Andy heard Mary in his earphone. "Andy, we checked. The apartment was leased two weeks ago. They paid for a year in advance. Obviously, they are using the local team to be the front."

"This place is empty. Nobody here," Andy said.

"Look around, Andy. Check the drawers, the refrigerator. They may have left something for you to see. We already picked up the driver who dropped you off. Same story. Some young woman approached him and paid him a hundred dollars to pick you up and drop you off. She told him it was a surprise party for you."

"A surprise party alright. These guys have a sick sense of humor." Andy proceeded to look around the apartment but found nothing

in the living room or bathrooms. In the master bedroom, he opened
the drawer in the nightstand. There was an envelope with Andy's
name on it. He opened it and saw a piece of paper that said:

> Mr. Sykes,
>   Go to the nightstand on the other side of the bed. You will
> find a cell phone. Use it. That will be the only one you will use.
>   Take your old cell phone and your earphone and leave
> them on the living room table.
>   Do it now, please. We are watching.
>   Then leave the room. Go downstairs. Leave the building.
> Wait for instructions.

Andy took a quick picture of the note and sent it to Mary, praying he was discrete. If they had cameras in the room, they might also
have hidden microphones, he figured.

Andy went to the kitchen, found a glass, filled it with water from
the faucet, and took a sip. He then leaned over the note, pretending
he was reading it again. He took out the small earphones, put them
in his mouth, swallowed them, and drank the water to chase them
down.

He went to the living room and placed his cell phone on the
coffee table. Then he left the apartment, took the elevator to the
lobby, and left the building. Andy hesitated once outside, not sure
what was going to happen. He kept looking around, disconnected
from Mary and his support, waiting.

43

MARY, THE GENERAL, and Natalie were following Andy very closely. The only access now was the tracker inside of him. They were hopeful the kidnappers would not suspect or find out what happened. Andy had to convince them he never had the earphones.

General Masoud told them, "We may have a positive ID of a Russian who fits the description and the locations. The security guard and the staff of the coffee shop confirmed his identity. He seems to have multiple locations, obviously moving around often. My security team found three locations under different names, all subleased at various times to families, none of them Russians. The team is investigating two more sites."

———

They watched as Andy had left the building. The new cell phone buzzed, and he picked it up.

"Mr. Sykes, we know about the earphones that you swallowed and did not leave on the table, as we instructed you. A reminder, Mr. Sykes: we already know all your moves. Don't waste any more time; just follow our instructions."

Andy was taken aback. They had to have cameras inside the apartment. "I did not have any earphones. All my communications were on the cell phone I left behind. Now where is my wife? I demand to speak to her." Andy decided to continue his charade. He wanted them to know he was upset.

"Not yet, Mr. Sykes."

"Bullshit. No more of this. If you want my help, I need to talk to my wife now. I mean it," Andy said.

There was a pause. They knew Andy was serious. "Okay, Mr. Sykes, we will get Mrs. Sykes on the phone."

It took a couple of minutes. "Andy, is that you?" Jennifer said, her voice clear and strong.

"Jenn, are you okay? Are they treating you well?"

"I am okay. I am okay. Please take care of yourself. We will be together soon," Jennifer said.

"Alright, Mr. Sykes? Your wife is fine." The kidnapper was back on the line. "We want you to walk to the next block. There is a hotel with taxis lined up in front. Take a taxi. We will give you the address once you are in the cab." He hung up before Andy could say anything.

Andy walked over to the hotel and grabbed the first taxi in front. The driver asked, "Where to?" Andy told him, "I'll let you know" and got inside the cab.

The cell phone buzzed, and Andy was given the address, which he then gave to the driver. The driver said, "That's in Sharjah, the neighboring city and emirate." Andy didn't say anything.

———

Mary and others were tracking Andy. They could tell he was in a vehicle. The general's team, scattered about, were also tracking Andy's movement in the cab.

"They are going to Sharjah," the general told Mary. "That's not a problem; my team can operate there." He made sure the head of security in Sharjah was notified.

———

The taxi stopped in front of a villa in a residential area. Andy got out, and his cell phone buzzed. "Please walk to the house three doors away with red entry doors and walk in," the kidnapper said.

"I am not walking in anywhere until I see evidence that my wife is released," Andy said.

"You will see the evidence once you walk in."

"No. Evidence of her safety first."

"Mr. Sykes, just walk in the outside gate. There will be no guards present. There will be a computer screen. Turn it on. It will show where your wife is," the kidnapper said.

Andy stopped moving; he hesitated, looking around and unsure. He had no choice. He walked over to the villa with the red door. He pushed open the outside gate and left it open. No guards were around. Jut to the right, there was a laptop. He pressed the on button, and images appeared.

Sure enough, there was Jennifer in a cab in front of their hotel. Andy saw her leave the cab and walk toward the hotel entry. Just then, he heard the click of the front gate locking. Two masked men burst out of the house with guns. One placed a hood on Andy's head; the other tied his hands.

He heard a car or truck pull up in front, and he was pushed in. It must have been a van. It drove off. Andy was in total darkness and silence.

———

As soon as they saw Jennifer on camera entering the hotel, the general immediately ordered his team to get there and make sure she was safe. Mary told Natalie and Bob to go and stay with Jennifer and find out what they could. Mary was staying with the general.

The tracking signal suddenly stopped. Mary and the general realized Andy was being transported in an electronically secure van. Both realized that Andy was completely on his own. The team had a few hours, maximum, to locate and rescue him.

44

THE GENERAL BROUGHT Mary to his office to talk.

"Mary, we have a mole, either in your organization or one of the companies, someone who has clear access to and knows all our moves. Our officer, the ringleader, did not know or divulge Mrs. Sykes's activities. There are too many strange happenings and events that lead me to think the CIA has to be involved. What are you not sharing with me?" The general looked at his old friend, waiting for answers.

Mary was quiet. She looked at the general and leaned forward. "Masoud, you are right; there are some things I have discovered since arriving here that I have not shared with you. I fully intended to but couldn't because I still don't know the full story. I still have too many questions."

"Mary, you should not keep this away from me; you are here in Dubai, on my turf. There is no excuse; besides, whatever it is, I can help. I don't want surprises, Mary. Is the CIA involved in some operation in the UAE that I don't know about and should know about?" the general said.

"You are right, Masoud. Of course I should have told you. Here is what we have found. There appears to be a rogue operation going on by some executives of CTC, maybe Sebastian Corporation, and maybe Pinnacle; we don't know yet. It is centered around the new hardware, the server, proposed by CTC. The server may be more powerful than proposed and may be used for more offensive purposes than planned. More importantly, whatever is planned is in violation of US national security," Mary said.

"Is the CIA involved?"

"No, we are not," Mary told him.

"Are you sure? It may not be your unit. How about other operations?" the general asked.

Mary hesitated. She stood up and walked toward the bookcases in the room and then turned around. "No, I am not sure," she finally said. She told the general about the boxes being stolen and the roles played by her team. She also told him about Bill Sorenson and Tyler Grant. She trusted General Masoud. They needed to work together.

Mary said, "I'll be going to the US consulate, where both Tyler and Bill are being questioned, and then will get back to continue monitoring the events around the kidnapping."

"Mary, you mentioned there may be individuals in Pinnacle involved. Do you know who?"

"Not sure yet, Masoud."

"Who do you suspect? I need to know."

"It is best we wait until I have a clearer picture, maybe after I question the two Americans. I will let you know when I get back." Mary left his office and headed to the US consulate.

45

MARY WENT DIRECTLY to the secure room in the US consulate. She was directed by the deputy director to prepare for a call with the director. She was accompanied by Major Garfield, the ranking security officer in the consulate with the necessary security clearances.

Mary and the major were waiting in the room when the screen came on. The director of the CIA and Tim Paterson, the deputy director, appeared onscreen. On a separate screen, the secretary of defense appeared.

"Good morning, Mary. Please give us the latest development," the director said.

Mary straightened up in her chair. She knew the seriousness of the situation to have both the director and the secretary on the call.

"Yes, sir. Jennifer Sykes, the wife of the architect, has been released; the kidnappers have her husband now. The UAE security agency has narrowed down the identity of the kidnappers to be Russian. We think they may be Russian mafia, but we're not sure if they are sanctioned or approved by their government," Mary said.

"I called the director of Russian Intelligence; he assured me they knew nothing of the kidnapping. They are to follow up and get back to me. What are the kidnappers demanding?" the director said.

"So far, nothing, sir. Our assumption is that they are in possession of one of the boxes, the new server. We don't know yet how they got it or who gave it to them and why. The CTC executive, Bill Sorenson, who was in possession of both boxes, claims they were both stolen from him here in Dubai," Mary said.

"We know about the two boxes. Tim briefed us. We are questioning the two executives from CTC and Sebastian. So far, they claim the additional server was more powerful, to be used only if needed. They both know they are in violation of national security," the director said.

Mary looked surprised that Tim had shared information from an ongoing investigation without verification.

"That is what we are hearing so far, sir. We don't buy it; we believe there is much more to this than we have been told," Mary said.

"Mary, Major Garfield, I agree. We were reluctant to issue the license to CTC for the commercial use of this sensitive hardware for a foreign entity. We agreed because the foreign entity is a strong ally, CTC has been a loyal and reliable partner, and our own desire was to produce an effective cyber defense. The way this whole thing is unfolding stinks. We have to stop it, whatever it is. We can't allow this hardware to be used against us." The secretary of defense was emphatic. "Major, if you cannot retrieve it, you must destroy it. We are going to get to the bottom of this."

"Mary, I want daily reporting at a minimum. I will share the information with the director," Tim Patterson said.

"Ms. Tobias, I am here to stress the point that the box must not, and I stress, must not get lost. We have to get it back here without any delay," the secretary of defense said.

"Mary, one more thing. From what we have been told, one of the boxes is the legitimate hardware that was planned for the building. The other is enhanced. We believe that the kidnappers want and have the one that is enhanced," the director said.

"How? We were assured by Cyber Technologies that what they have is *not* the enhanced. Who made the switch? This changes everything, sir," Mary said.

"The two executives of Cyber Technologies and Sebastian Corporation have been arrested. They are in custody. They managed to make the switch using people loyal to them on the ground in Dubai. There will be more arrests," the director said.

46

WHEN THE VIDEO call ended, Mary stood up and asked Major Garfield to join her in getting an update from their team who was questioning Tyler Grant and Bill Sorenson. Rusty and two others were questioning Tyler, who was still bandaged. In an adjoining room, Bill was being questioned by another security officer. No lawyers were around. Mary sent a text to Rusty and the security officer to come out for debriefing. They both did.

"Tyler told us that he took the box from the abandoned warehouse. He said Bill gave him the key and the location where the box was hidden. He said Bill wanted him to keep it if something happened to Bill. He told us he was working directly with Bill's boss, the senior VP of the company, who instructed Tyler to take the box and keep it in his hotel room. He also said that Bill's technical director was with him, keeping an eye on Bill. He shared with him about the box location. That night, he found the box was missing from his hotel room. He claims he told Bill's boss. He swears he knows nothing about the Russians. He's adamant he is telling us the truth," Rusty reported.

"Did you bring the Cyber Technologies team member in for questioning?" Mary asked.

"Yes, he is here being questioned."

"How about Bill?"

"He admits to the unauthorized introduction of and attempt to use the box in the project. He has named others involved, both in the US and here. He swears he does not know anything about who stole the box, how the Russians wound up with it, or their intentions."

"Do you think Bill's assistant stole and sold the box to the Russians?"

"So far, the technical assistant insists that he hasn't. But he admitted that he knew Tyler had it in his room."

47

THE VAN CAME to a stop. Andy heard the door opening and movement of equipment on metal. He felt a hand help him up and move him to some place. He was walking on some sort of metal walkway. A door opened, and Andy was guided inside. The hood on his head was removed.

He was in a large room, no windows and padded walls made of some kind of material. This was a secure room. No electronic signals. Nobody from Andy's side knew where he was; he was on his own. "Not a comforting thought," Andy muttered to himself. "But at least Jennifer is safe."

Two men with ski masks were in the room. "Hello, Mr. Sykes. As promised, your wife is back in the hotel. If you work with us, you will join her in a short time."

"Okay, thank you for releasing my wife. But you are making a serious mistake. I have told you I don't have any information or knowledge about this black box. I don't even know what the damn thing looks like. I don't know how I can possibly help you." Andy was shouting.

"Mr. Sykes, we know who you are. We know your skills. You are an expert in AI application of cybersecurity in buildings. That is why you were selected," the tall kidnapper said.

"I know buildings. I know how to program how the building should function, how to connect the pieces, how to make it function efficiently, how to make it come alive. What I don't know is cyberse-curity and how that fits. This is the domain of Cyber Technologies. I don't know how the damn thing works. Their work is classified. One more thing: you both know that, by now, security forces of both countries are searching for me. They will find you. Don't make it any worse; let me go," Andy said in controlled anger.

"That is our point, Mr. Sykes. You must suspect that CTC has not shared the true purpose of their cyber program. You have expressed concerns. You are not satisfied with their explanations. We know what is going on. We also know they need you. We have a very short timeframe to get the box activated. We need the code. You have the code." The tall kidnapper stopped and stared at Andy with the confidence of superiority.

"National security forces have been mobilized to find us; they will, sooner or later. We have no more than three hours to get this done, for us to release you, and we all leave. If we are found, none of us will survive; that includes you, Mr. Sykes," he added. "Don't bull-shit us. We know you know the code. Activate it; your life depends on it. We will leave you with the box and a computer, and we will be back in one hour." The tall kidnapper appeared to be in charge.

"Wait, wait!" Andy screamed as they left the room.

Andy was alone, staring at the black steel box. He stood up and started pacing in the secure cell. Andy the architect was transform-ing into Andy the analyst. He was muttering, talking to himself.

"I will run out of time. Either way, I will be killed, I am con-vinced. I know I am screwed. My only hope is they find me very soon. Then what? These guys are not going to give up without a fight. There has to be a way. Think, Andy, think," he muttered.

He kept staring at the box. "What is this thing capable of?"

48

MARY WENT INTO the interrogation room where Bill Sorenson was. "Bill, we are running out of time. They have Andy. They will kill him if we can't rescue him within the next hour, two hours, max. I want answers. Now. You said that Tyler was the only person who knew where the first box was that you say was stolen, correct?"

"Yes."

"Tyler confirms he took it but swears it was taken from his hotel room. Who did you tell that the box was stolen in the first place?"

"The only person I told was the CEO of Pinnacle, Elias Khoury."

"When did you tell him?"

"He was with me when I discovered the box was gone."

"Was there anyone else you told?"

"My boss, Jeff Milbank, the senior VP of Cyber Technologies."

"Why would Tyler steal the box? To sell it to the Russians?"

"I am not sure. I don't think he would sell it to the Russians. My guess is he was working for my boss. He ordered him. I had expressed my concerns about the whole operation."

"How did Tyler and the person who attacked him in the apartment building know where you hid the second box?"

"I don't know."

"You must know."

"I may have been followed," Bill whispered.

"Not good enough. Why this elaborate scheme to hide the box in the first place?"

"I was worried it would fall into the wrong hands."

"Why?"

Bill paused and took a deep breath. "The two boxes are identical except for one difference. There is no fake box. Both are designed as a deterrent to cyberattacks. Both have defense capabilities. Both have the abilities to track the attacker, penetrate and hack their system. The one major difference is one is programmed to become a lethal cyber weapon later at our choosing."

"Mr. Sorenson, you have been played. The box that was stolen, the one the Russians have now, was the one that can be converted into a lethal weapon. This information came from the military. They have your boss and others under arrest. My orders are to retrieve the box or destroy it," Mary said. Bill froze. "Now, one more time, who knew about the apartment?"

"Tyler knew I had the apartment. He did not know what was hidden there."

"If Tyler was working with your boss, who knew there were two boxes, he may have ordered Tyler to search the apartment in case the box was hidden there. Right?" Mary said.

"Yes, that is possible."

"While there searching, he was attacked. The place was ransacked. The attacker either knew there was another box in the apartment, or he was following Tyler."

"Yes, that makes sense."

"Now listen, Bill. I need the name of the person who gave the box to the Russians. He is the same person who stole the box from Tyler's hotel room and attacked him in the apartment. You must have some suspicion as to who that may be. The only person that all the evidence points to is Mr. Khoury. He was part of this scheme, wasn't he?"

"He introduced the cyber system to this project. He was offered a generous commission. However, he was adamant it was not to be used as a lethal weapon. If I had to guess, it has to be someone within his organization or maybe a member of the board," Bill said.

Mary suddenly rushed out of the room. She took out her cell phone and called Natalie, who was in the car with Bob and Jennifer, heading to General Masoud's headquarters. Jennifer had insisted she be part of any decision regarding Andy. The general agreed.

Mary told Natalie, "Get the names from Bob of all the people with technical knowledge who have talked to the architects about the project since they arrived in Dubai."

Bob gave her the names.

49

MARY DIALED THE number for General Masoud and told him she was on her way to join him. She gave him two names of people to bring in for questioning.

He told her, "I will right away. We have the locations narrowed down to a few where Andy may be held. My team has questioned the coffee shop owner and many suspected members of the Russian mafia, and they reviewed exhaustive camera records throughout the city. They have identified several homes, apartments, and warehouses. They have already searched many and have it narrowed down to two villas and a warehouse."

Jennifer, Bob, and Natalie were all there with the general, following the images on multiple screens.

Before Mary joined them, she dialed the number for the CIA director. He answered immediately, and she gave him a brief status report.

"Sir, we may be running out of time. May I suggest another call from you to the head of the Russian Security? Let them know that the Russians are still holding an American hostage and request they demand his release immediately. They must know or have a way of knowing who they are in Dubai," Mary said.

"Mary, I am ahead of you. I already have. He assured me he

knows nothing about it yet. He promised to check into it and get back to me."

"Thank you, sir."

"Call me with updates. My priority is freeing Andy Sykes and recovering the box or destroying it. Do whatever it takes."

"Yes, sir."

———

Mary joined the group. She went directly to Jennifer, held her hand, and asked how she was doing. Jennifer was genuinely pleased to see Mary. She gave her a hug and held her hand. She looked haggard, and tears were in her eyes.

"We are going to bring Andy out. No matter what. I promise you," Mary said.

On the large screen, Mary was watching security forces mobilized around a house in Sharjah. It was one of the places that security forces had targeted. Streets within several blocks around the house were blocked to traffic. The special security unit was getting mobilized to storm the house, when in position. The order had to come from the general.

The general went back to the surveillance screens. His security people were positioned and waiting for his orders. They were a block away from the house, hidden from view.

Waiting and watching the screen with the others, the general noticed Jennifer, poised and completely focused. He was impressed with her strength and composure. He stood beside her and said, "Mrs. Sykes, we will not do anything that places your husband in danger. We are committed to getting him out safely. Rest assured."

"Thank you very much, General Masoud. That is very reassuring. Thank you," Jennifer said.

As he was watching the screen with the others, he turned and saw the chairman of Pinnacle walking slowly toward him with his cane. Ayman and his wife, Hania, were with him. The chairman had requested that the couple join them to support Mrs. Sykes. Hania immediately went to Jennifer and held her for a long time. No words were necessary.

"Any change?" the chairman asked.

"Our team is ready to storm one of the homes we suspect they are in. They are waiting for my orders."

On the screen, they could see the security forces surrounding the house with armored vehicles. A security member, one of the leaders, stepped outside the vehicle with a loudspeaker.

"You are surrounded. Please leave the house with your hands up. You will not be harmed. I repeat, leave the house with your hands up," the officer said.

The message was repeated several times. No response at all. He ordered his team and the armored vehicles to move forward, much closer to the house, and repeated the announcement again.

The team put on their gas masks and moved forward. Several gas canisters were shot through the windows. As the gas engulfed the building, the team rushed in with guns drawn.

Several minutes went by. Jennifer was holding on to Hania, when the team leader's voice came through the speaker in the war room. "There is no one here. The house is empty. No furniture at all." Jennifer was relieved. *Andy is still safe.*

"We have two more locations left. One is also a warehouse. I am confident this is where they are holding Mr. Sykes. We already have teams on their way. We are determined to keep the operation as low-key as we can. We don't want the press involved."

50

GENERAL MASOUD TOLD Mary he had the two Pinnacle men in custody, being questioned. Joseph Ferguson, the technical director, and Mounir Al Misri, the financial director for Pinnacle Enterprises, were in separate rooms.

She told the general, "I have to go back to the consulate to assist in the interrogations of Tyler Grant and Bill Sorenson, but I'll be back. I ask that no action be taken regarding the rescue operations without my knowledge." Then she left.

The general watched the questioning of the two company directors. No new revelations. Both were pleading ignorance. He had ordered a detailed review of the two men's backgrounds, their history, and current activities. He was expecting the reports at any time.

An assistant approached the general with the reports he had ordered. He read the summary. Then he immediately went to the interrogation room and ordered the two interrogators to come out. He gave them the reports with specific instructions.

He ordered Mounir Al Misri released but said to hold Joseph Ferguson for further questioning. Then he went back to the war room and asked the chairman of Pinnacle to join him in his office.

"Abu Haider, we have been questioning your company technical and financial directors. We let Mounir go, but we kept Mr. Ferguson for further questioning. We found disturbing communications between him and people we suspect. We don't have all the facts, but I wanted you to know," the general said.

51

ANDY CONTINUED STARING at the black box, touching it, feeling it, holding it. The computer they gave him was sitting there helplessly, waiting for an operator. Andy knew the codes to activate, but he was reluctant to do so.

"How do I even begin to figure this out? If I activate it, they may kill me; if I keep stalling and run out of time, they may also kill me. It is hopeless. Shit." Andy was mumbling to himself again.

"Time is running out. They will be coming in soon. What do I tell them with nothing to give them? I need more time. More time for what? To stall? To delay? For how long?" Andy was pacing, talking to himself. He was known to stay cool under pressure, but he was thinking he may be losing it.

Andy kept staring—staring and thinking.

"Looking at this highly sensitive, high-security, classified piece of equipment owned and protected by the US government, how can they possibly allow it to be in this room with me, controlled by a bunch of thugs?" His mind was racing. "This machine has to be completely protected and secure. There probably is no way to activate it without extremely complex protocol. No way." Andy was searching, talking to himself.

Then it hit him. The lightbulb came on like a bolt of lightning. "Of course, of course. Now I remember what Bill told me." Andy started pacing faster, talking to himself loudly.

"Now what do I do? How do I convince these crazy bastards? Even if they kill me, they get nothing. Bottom line, they get nothing, no matter what. They either get killed and me with them, or they spend the rest of their days in prison."

Andy started laughing. He wasn't sure if it was the laughter of resignation or desperation. The reality of his condition smacked him straight in the face.

"Hello, Mr. Sykes. Why are you laughing? We hope it is because you managed to access the box," the kidnapper said, as he and his shorter partner walked in.

"Well, gentlemen, it is not quite that," Andy said.

"Then share with us, Mr. Sykes. We are completely out of time."

"Well, gentlemen, I hate to give you the bad news, but I cannot activate the box with this worthless computer you have given me. I have tried everything."

"What are you talking about? You must be delirious. Your time is up. This is your last warning. You'd better—"

"Or what? Or what, gentlemen? Now you listen to me. I hate to give you the bad news, but I cannot open it this way. I need either a more powerful computer or some tools to allow me to physically open it and activate it. Your choice. But no matter what I do, open this box or not, there is no way out for you." Andy was done.

"What are you talking about?" They started laughing. "We have you, and we have the box," the tall one said. "Worst case, we kill you, and we take the box. We have experts who will be able to access it. It may take time. We have time. But you will be dead. So, for the last time, Mr. Sykes," he said as he pulled out his gun and pointed it at Andy's head. "For the last time, are you going to open this machine or not?"

Andy stared at him, unfazed. He knew they were not going to shoot him, at least not yet. "Okay, gentlemen, right now, as we speak, the entire UAE security force is looking for me. By now, they know who you are, what you do, and where you live. They know every place you have lived. I would not be surprised if they crashed in right now. In other words, you cannot get away. To complicate matters for you, I have figured this machine out. I cannot open it this way. I have to physically open it. There is no other way. The only way is to physically access it. Get me the tools."

"What kind of tools?" the big man said.

"An electric drill that I can use to drill through quarter-inch steel and a twelve-inch screwdriver," Andy said.

"How much time do you need?"

"With the right tools, fifteen minutes."

They looked at each other, and the one who appeared to be in charge said, "We will be back with the tools." Then they left the room.

52

MARY WALKED INTO the room where Jason Bower, the technical director, was being questioned. She turned off the intercom system and asked the questioner to leave the room.

"Good morning, Jason. I am Mary Tobias with the CIA. I understand you have some important information to share."

"Yes, I do. This whole fiasco has become totally out of control, just as I predicted. I warned them from day one."

"Who did you warn?"

"I warned both Mr. Sorenson and Mr. Milbank."

"Your boss and the senior vice president of Cyber Technologies?"

"Yes."

"What was your warning?"

"The way they were planning this was all wrong. I told them to completely separate the two efforts. Installing a cyber technology initiative that had offensive capabilities should be treated separately."

"Was that because it was a lethal weapon?"

"That was before I found out they were substituting it with the potential weapon. It was illegal."

"Did you share that with anybody?"

"No, I didn't. I was too deep into it."

"Did you figure this out when you arrived in Dubai?"

"Yes."

"How did you determine what was happening?"

"Bill Sorenson trusted me. He brought one of the boxes to me back in Boston and asked me to keep it in a safe place until he was ready to take it with us to Dubai."

"Where did you keep it?"

"In my home, in the basement."

"You were dealing with highly sensitive and secure hardware. How did you get away with treating it so nonchalantly?" Mary leaned forward, closer to his face.

"Bill assured me he had authorization. The box was useless without the codes to activate it. It was for commercial application, and it would self-destruct if not used properly," Jason said.

"What did you do then?" Mary said.

"I kept it until we left for Dubai," Jason replied.

"But it was the planned box, not the altered?" Mary asked.

"That is right."

"When did you find out there was another box, a much more advanced and potentially offensive one?"

"Bill Sorenson told me. He was quite disturbed by it."

"Did you steal the box?" Mary asked.

"No way, absolutely not," Jason replied.

"Were you reporting Mr. Sorenson's activities back to Mr. Milbank?"

"No, I was loyal to Bill."

"Did you work for and report back to the Department of Defense?"

"No, I did not."

"The CIA? Were you reporting to the CIA?" Mary asked.

Jason refused to answer.

53

THE TWO MEN came back with a box of tools and an electric drill that could drill through the steel plate. "Here is what you asked for. Before you start any work, tell us what you are planning to do," the big guy said.

"As I told you, I know what I am doing. Nothing inside will be damaged. You'll see." Andy grabbed the drill and found the right size bit that would punch a hole through the plate no smaller than three-eighths of an inch. He set the drill and the box down with the long side vertically up on the table. He marked a spot with a pencil approximately in the middle of the twelve-inch square plate. Then he grabbed the drill.

"Wait. What are you doing? You will damage it," the leader said.

"No, I will not. Please trust me. I know what I'm doing." Andy turned the box on the opposite side and placed a mark in the middle of the plate. He was praying and mumbling to himself, hoping he was right about what would happen.

Andy started to drill, when the short guy screamed, "Stop!" Andy stopped drilling. "He is going to ruin this machine, I know it. I will kill you if you do, I will," he shouted.

"Listen, both of you. There is no other option to activate this box. You either get me the computer that I need or let me physically open it. I will be very careful not to damage it, but I can't guarantee it. There is a third option: give up. Nobody has been hurt yet; let me negotiate for you and guarantee your safety," Andy said.

The short and stocky Russian aimed his gun directly at Andy's face, but the big guy pulled him back and told him to back off. "Okay, Mr. Sykes, go ahead. We are watching," the leader said.

It took a few tries getting through the plate and getting rid of the metal shavings. Andy turned the box up to the bottom plate and drilled the same size hole. "Now I want you to watch closely." He grabbed the long, quarter-inch-diameter screwdriver, inserted it very slowly into the hole, and started to push it through. The screwdriver touched a metal surface. Immediately, there was an explosion inside the box, and black smoke started coming out from both ends. The box was self-destructing. Andy jumped backward and fell flat on his back.

The two men looked at the box with horror and anger. The smaller guy lunged at Andy; he started screaming and punching him, cursing him in Russian. Andy took a few good punches before the big guy grabbed his partner and pulled him away from Andy, who stood up, coughing blood.

"You are a dead man. You are going down with us," the short kidnapper said.

The other guy was frantic, pacing, coming unglued. "I am going to kill you," he kept repeating.

"Listen to me. Listen," Andy yelled. They became quiet. "You kidnapped my wife. Now you have me. I did not ask for this. You did. And here we are. Now the three of us are in this together, whether we like it or not. We all know the entire police force is looking for us. It is just a matter of time. They may be outside right now. The only chance you have to survive is to work with me and trust me. I know if they come crashing in here, I will be killed, like you. You can give up and surrender. Maybe they will just deport you. Maybe prison and then deport you. Both are better options than dying. Remember, nobody has been killed yet." Andy was hoping they'd listen.

They looked at each other, speaking Russian. The big guy turned around. "No, that will not work. They will crucify us. I know they will. We need assurance. We need a guarantee. We will leave the country but no prison. I will call your wife. She will convince them. Your life will be our passport."

"That will not work. Trust me. They may still believe you have the box and it is safe. They also need me for the project. Let me try to negotiate an exit for you and for my release," Andy said.

"Okay, we will do it your way. If you fail, I will do it my way," the tall kidnapper said after a long pause.

"I will not fail. Now I need my cell phone. You have it," Andy said.

"We can't let you use your cell phone; they will know your location."

"Alright, give me your phone. I also need mine. I need to get a number," Andy said as he rubbed his jaw.

"You are not calling your wife?" the short kidnapper asked.

"No, I am not. That will be later," Andy replied.

54

MARY WAS WATCHING the images on the big screen. Security forces, armored vehicles—a small army waiting for their orders. Mary looked at Jennifer, who was covering her mouth with both hands. The chairman was focused but calm.

General Masoud leaned over and told Mary he was ready to give the order, when her cell phone buzzed. It showed no numbers. She turned it off. It immediately rang again. She hesitated and then answered.

"Mary, it's me, Andy." Mary immediately waved to the general, signaling to hold. He stood still, waiting.

"Andy, where are you?"

"I am being held hostage. Don't know where, but I am sure it is a house. I am using their cell phone."

"Thank God you are safe. What's happening? What do they want?"

"Listen, Mary. They know it is over. They'd rather go down fighting and be killed with me than surrender. I convinced them to give me a chance to negotiate terms. They have agreed. I don't have much time."

"What are the terms?" Mary said.

"Safe passage to leave the country."

"Andy, that is a tall order. I don't think General Masoud will accept."

"You must convince him. If you can't, I will be killed along with them, and the box will be destroyed."

"Alright, let me talk to General Masoud."

"No. I have to be in on the call. Who else is there with you?"

"Jennifer, Bob, Ayman, his wife, and the chairman of Pinnacle."

"Bring the general and the chairman with you to a private room and put me on speaker."

"Okay, stay on the line. Give me a minute."

Mary walked over to the general and the chairman, motioning to them to follow her. She asked General Masoud for a private room.

"Andy, I have General Masoud and the chairman with me. Please go ahead."

"General, Mr. Chairman, I will get to the point. There isn't much time. They will release me if they are allowed to leave the country. No trial. No prison."

"Impossible. We can't do that. That is just not possible," the general said.

"You have the authority, General. Anything is possible. Let's be logical. A trial should be the last thing you want. How are you and the two governments going to explain the controversy around cybersecurity? This will come out in the trial," Andy said persuasively. "Think about it. Not only am I saved, but no one is killed, and the box is returned."

The general looked at Mary for her opinion. She agreed with Andy. "A trial would be harmful. The matter needs to be settled quietly."

The chairman was listening to the discussions. "Andy, I am glad you are safe. My priority is to move forward with Al Bustan. There is some housecleaning I have to do. The US government has to take care of its own," the chairman said. "General Masoud, I share your concerns. However, I do agree with Andy; this should be handled properly. We need to end this, General. We need to free Mr. Sykes without any bloodshed."

"Alright. Tell them we accept. Here are my conditions. They give us a list of all their thugs in Dubai. They all depart the country and are not allowed to return. I want a list of local participants in their criminality, the location of all their facilities, and they release you immediately, unharmed. Andy, my people are outside the villa. I need to make sure it is the right one," the general said.

"Thank you. I will get back to you." Andy hung up and looked at his two captors, who were both listening. "Gentlemen, you will not get a better deal. You know you don't have too many options. They also have to know, as do I, who helped them. What is your answer?"

The two were pacing and talking. They knew it was over. "Alright, Mr. Sykes, we will accept the conditions. We want guarantees in writing that they will not come after us through our government," the big man said.

"I need the address of this place," Andy said. He dialed Mary's cell number again, using their phone. Mary answered immediately. "They accept. Two conditions: the agreement is to be in writing and no follow-up or sharing any of the information with other countries, especially their native country," Andy told Mary and the others who were listening.

"Mr. Sykes, this is General Masoud. I will prepare and sign the agreement as requested. I will have one of my men give it to you at the entry. In exchange, they must provide me the list of members of their organization and their collaborators. They have twenty-four hours to leave the country."

55

ALL EYES WERE on the front door of the house in Sharjah. Mary was standing next to General Masoud. Chairman Marwan was watching the giant screen with Ayman. Jennifer was holding Hania's arm. Their attention was on the screen with images of the front door of the villa and of the troops surrounding it. The general had his phone in his hand, coordinating with his commander on the ground.

"Ahmed, go ahead," the general said to his commander, Captain Ahmed Sulaiman.

The captain picked up his loudspeaker. "Come out one at a time with your hands up. You will be unharmed if you follow my orders. No sudden moves. Hands up. Come out now."

The captain waited. There was no movement. He called out again on the loudspeaker, demanding that whoever was in the house leave immediately with their hands up.

Five minutes later, the front door opened. A short and stocky man dressed in all black emerged with his hands up. He looked hesitant but defiant. He stopped outside the door and waited.

The second Russian emerged with both hands up, also dressed all in black. He was a big man, tall with broad shoulders. He stood outside the door next to his partner.

Jennifer held on to Hania, waiting for Andy to appear. It was only a few minutes later, but felt like an hour to Jennifer, when Andy appeared. He raised his hands. His face was all bruised. He stood on the side, looking at the troops and the armored vehicles. He was smiling.

The captain started moving slowly toward the three with three policemen behind him. He was within ten feet of the Russians, when the crowd in the war room watched with horror as two shots from nowhere struck each of them. They collapsed immediately.

Andy jumped to the floor, trying to hide. The captain moved quickly, grabbed Andy, and pulled him away from the scene. His troops dispersed, not knowing where the sniper was. He had to be in one of the villas or high-rises close by.

The captain pushed Andy into his car and told the driver to take him immediately to headquarters. He ordered his team to cordon off the area and start searching for the sniper.

The general kept staring at the screen. He motioned to his assistant and said, "Mobilize whatever is needed and start searching all potential buildings. Jennifer, Andy is safe and on his way to headquarters."

"This changes everything, General," Mary said.

"I know."

"Where is the box? I did not see the box. General, please order your captain to go inside and retrieve it," Mary said.

The general called the captain, who was already inside the villa. He covered the box, still emanating black smoke, and went outside. He uncovered the box and lifted it for the general to see.

"Oh, no, the box has self-destructed. That is Andy's doing. That is how he maneuvered the situation. We have to contain this until we find out what's going on," Mary said.

"I have already ordered no leaks or disclosures. The official story is this is a drug raid," the general said. "These two Russians were killed to silence them. Mary, let's go to my office. We need to talk."

Once there, the general closed the door behind her. "I need

answers, Mary. This whole operation smells. I smell CIA all over this. Iranians and Russians would not act this way. Not here. Not now. This is a cover-up to protect some people. Mary, what are you hiding from me?"

"Masoud, I assure you this killing is not CIA or any other US government agency. I am as disturbed and perplexed as you are. It is clear whoever ordered these killings has much at stake and much to hide. What I have shared fully with you is the involvement of private US contractors in a rogue operation regarding this project. We know who they are and what we assume to be their objectives. The group includes rogue government officials and UAE individuals," Mary said.

"I want details of everything you know, who is involved, and what is the plan. It has to be significant for them to take this kind of risk. I want names. I have mobilized my team. It is obvious these two men were killed to silence them. We will find the shooter. You make your inquiries, and we will confer then. For now, we need to interview the architect," the general said.

56

ANDY WAS IN the police car with the officer escorting him to head-quarters. An escort vehicle was close behind. The medics had treated the bruises on his face, and he looked reasonably present-able.

Arriving at headquarters, he saw the reception crowd: the gen-eral, the chairman, Mary, Natalie, and Bob. Jennifer already left the group and started running toward him with tears in her eyes. She flung her arms around him. Andy held her tight and would not let go. He buried his face in her chest with tears in his eyes also.

The rest waited for the couple and gave them the privacy they needed. Then Bob came over and gave Andy a hug. The atmosphere was one of relief. They all walked in the building, and Mary and the general came over.

"Andy, thank God you are safe. This has been a very trying time for both of you. Unfortunately, we need to get a briefing from you now. The situation is volatile. We have to get on top of this. Sorry, Jennifer, but right now we need to talk alone with Andy; please bear with us. You may want to get back to the hotel. It will not be long. I'll drive Andy there when we're finished," Mary said.

"Of course. You need to interview Andy, but I will be there with him," Jennifer said.

"Mrs. Sykes, we can't do that; we simply can't. Please understand. We will bring Andy to the hotel very soon." Mary looked to the general, who nodded.

"Darling, that's okay. I will be fine. Please go back to the hotel with Bob," Andy said.

"I will be happy to drive you two back to the hotel," Natalie said.

"Alright, I'll go, but I have to tell you I am not very happy about it. Andy, demand answers for what we have gone through. Something stinks. We saw two men killed in front of our eyes." Jennifer turned around and joined Bob and Natalie.

Andy followed Mary and the general to his private conference room. "Andy, we are very sorry for the ordeal you have gone through. Your presence here should have been pleasant, focused on your new project. We will get to the bottom of this, I promise you. I need to ask you some questions about your kidnappers first," the general started.

"No, General, I have questions for you and Mary, and I demand answers. My wife and I have been held by thugs ready to kill us. We have no idea who they are or why they wanted us. Now we are caught up in some crazy terrorist scheme that involves your governments, the US and the UAE. All about some secret offensive weapon that you have assured us you know nothing about. A weapon for which we have been imprisoned and almost killed. I demand you tell me what the hell this is all about. Who is behind this? A black box that may not be what it seems. Russian mafia willing to risk their lives for it," Andy said.

"Andy, this is highly classified. I will explain and share what we know with you once we get at the bottom of this. We are questioning people. I will tell you everything once we know," Mary replied.

"We almost got killed because of this so-called classified thing. I demand to know, Mary. I have earned the right to know."

"Andy, you have been through an unimaginable ordeal. Most importantly, you are safe. I assure you neither government has anything to do with what has happened. I will share with you what we have discovered, almost all of it within the last couple of days. We have a rogue operation going on. It involves members of two US companies, CTC and Sebastian Corporation. We believe the players are operating on their own without the knowledge or approval of the companies they work for," Mary said. "We are not sure yet what their motive or objective is. Is it greed or some twisted ideology? We don't know; it may be both. We also suspect that others, both in the US and the UAE, may be involved. We are questioning all the people associated with this project."

"Is CTC, the company, driving this? Is Bill Sorenson the leader of the group?" Andy asked.

"He is definitely the implementer. Strings are being pulled by his superiors," Mary said.

"The assassination of the two Russians was obviously accomplished by a trained professional, most probably military. Any theories as to who may have given the order?"

"Andy, we will find out. You are correct; this is the work of a highly skilled professional assassin," Mary said.

"I have some questions for you now. Andy, you were the central figure. What exactly did they say they wanted you to do?" the general asked.

"After all the maneuvers to get me there, I was in a room in a villa, probably the same room that Jennifer was in. I was in the room with the black box. They wanted me to unlock and access it."

"Did they seem to know what was inside the box?" Mary asked.

"I had the feeling they were not quite sure what exactly the box was. They were convinced it was of great value," Andy said.

"What kind of value?" the general asked.

"It was clear to me they thought it was a cyber weapon of some kind."

"Andy, why did they think you could unlock the box?" Mary said.

"I think that was the assumption by everyone. To buy time, I kept telling them I had no clue. They wouldn't believe me. Some-how, someone must have told them I had the secret, the codes, or whatever it was they needed."

"Any hint who they were taking orders from?" Mary said.

"No, but what was telling was that they were under a timeline pressure. They kept telling me we were running out of time."

"Maybe they knew we were closing in on them."

"That was clear, but there seemed to be pressure from someone higher up."

"Then what happened? How did you convince them you could not unlock the box?" Mary asked.

"I had memorized the codes. I could have activated it. I didn't to buy time," Andy said.

"But you destroyed the box. How did you know to do that, and why destroy it?" the general said.

"Bill Sorenson told us in his briefing that the box had a self-de-struct mechanism. I calculated that if I activated the box, they would not have further use for me and kill me. If I destroyed it, I may have a better chance, at least they will not have the box," Andy said.

"How did you destroy it?" Mary said.

"I asked them to get me a drill and a screwdriver. They did. I drilled a hole in each end and ran the screwdriver through until it hit a plate. That did the trick I was hoping for," Andy said.

"What did they do?"

"They went nuts. The short guy was ready to kill me; he started punching me. The big guy pulled him away. I told them they were screwed and me with them. The only way out was to negotiate a surrender. You know the rest," Andy said.

The general stood up, came over, shook Andy's hand, and smiled. "Andy, you have balls," he said. "You and Jennifer need your privacy and a well-deserved rest. I will have my driver take you to your hotel."

57

MARY FOLLOWED THE general to his office. His top lieutenant was waiting. "What have we discovered about the shooter?" the general asked.

"We determined what building the shots came from. We reviewed the cameras in the area and saw the flash. It came from the twenty-second floor of a tower two blocks away, with a clear view of the villa," the lieutenant said. "We barricaded and locked down the building. There are four large apartments on the twenty-second floor. We checked each unit. Three were occupied, but no one saw or heard anything unusual. The unit where we believe the shooter was in was unoccupied, but we did see gunpowder residue on the windowsill where we believe the shooter was positioned. The unit is rented to a couple, both at work at the time of the shooting. We have them here at headquarters being questioned. They claim they have not given the key or permission to anyone to use their apartment, except for the wife's brother, who apparently stays with them from time to time."

"What are their nationalities?"

"He is Portuguese."

"And the wife?"

"She is Russian."

"What does her brother do?"

"He is a pilot with Aeroflot."

"Do we have a photograph of him?"

"Yes, sir, we do."

"Have we located him?"

"We have an APB out on him now. Nothing so far."

"Have you checked with Aeroflot?"

"He was scheduled to fly an hour ago but did not show up. They replaced him with another pilot."

"Did you contact the Russian Embassy?"

"Yes. They claim they have not heard from him."

"Have you checked the airport, airlines, train stations, highway cameras?"

"Yes, sir. Nothing yet."

"Okay, Lieutenant, keep pressing. Let me know as soon as you find anything."

"Yes, sir. I will. One more thing, General. The wife knew the two Russians who were shot. She may have been part of the group. The apartment they rented was to be close to the villa. She is under arrest for further questioning." He left.

General Masoud looked at Mary. "What do you think? Is the Russian government involved? A message to the mafia?" he asked.

"Maybe it's the mafia silencing the two," Mary said. "If it's the Russian government, they clearly don't want the publicity. It may be a message to the mafia to stay in line or else. The shooter may very well be with the mafia, taking orders from their security agency," Mary said.

The general was quiet for a few moments. "Mary, we may never find out. The shooter may have already slipped out using a different passport. He could be in Oman, on his way to Russia, or hiding somewhere away from Russia."

"How do we know for certain who was behind this? What if it is one of ours or yours using the Russians?" the general asked.

"Unfortunately, I believe you may be right. We may never find out. For now, we have a number of players from both sides that we need to question. I will go back to the consulate and start. You need to interrogate the people with Pinnacle. I'll call you later in the day," Mary said.

"Okay, Mary, but we have to have full and clear disclosure in finding all the facts. There is no other way. For now, the official story is that this whole operation is drug related."

"You have my word, Masoud."

58

MARY WENT DIRECTLY to the consulate. She instructed Natalie to meet her there, and they were back in the secure room with Bill Sorenson.

"Okay, Bill. Start from the top. What exactly was the plan? From the beginning," Mary stated.

"Our original plan was to supply Pinnacle with the most advanced cybersecurity hardware we have. The most sophisticated server to protect the project from cyberattacks. The server was the black box. Unknown to Pinnacle Enterprises and all the participants, we had a second black box made, identical to the original in all aspects. The only difference was an attachment inside the box that was invisible. It can be converted to a more powerful and lethal server that can literally dismantle any electronic equipment by reversing the cyberattack against the cyberattacker. Its value is its ability to focus and zero in on the target."

"It can perform simply by the additional capacity from the censors in the new building?" Mary asked.

"Yes."

"That's where the architect comes in?"

"Yes."

"Who was helping you locally?" she asked. "Who are your partners? Pinnacle's CEO, Mr. Khoury?"

"He only helped by getting us in on the project."

"Did you pay him?"

"We offered. He almost fired us. He took responsibility for what happened."

"Somebody higher up had to help you. Who was it?"

"It was the young board member from Pinnacle," Bill said.

"Why? Why risk a bright career? For what?"

"I don't know. My guess is he has a direct link to someone in Washington."

"Who?"

"I don't know."

"You must know," Mary insisted. "Who directed you to connect to the board member?"

"My boss, Jeff Milbank."

"What were his directions?"

"He directed me to work with the board member and follow his instructions regarding logistics."

"Did you?"

"I did not share where I hid the boxes."

"Why not?"

"I was nervous. I didn't trust what was going on."

"Why not?"

"There was something about the whole operation that disturbed me. I began to suspect the true nature of the plan."

"What did you think it was?"

"Something did not add up. The way it was run. They were too secretive about the true nature of this cyber offensive weapon."

"Did you share your concerns with anyone?"

"No, I did not. I shared some of my concerns with Jason, my technical director, but not fully. I asked him to keep one of the boxes in a safe place for me." Bill looked remorseful.

"Let me switch gears. Why did you and Jeff concoct this high-risk, illegal plan in the first place? Was it money? Some twisted ideology?" Mary prompted.

"This was all about money. If we proved the success of the server, we could market it globally," Bill said.

"How does Tyler Grant fit in? You told him where the box was. Why? Was he part of the group?"

"No, he was not. I worked with him on previous projects. I used him on this one. I simply asked him to help me out and keep it to himself. He did."

"Did he take the box?"

"He must have. I didn't realize until now that he was working for Jeff."

"He claims he had the box in his hotel room, where it was stolen. Who else would he know who would steal it?"

"I have no idea."

"How did Tyler know about the second box in your apartment?"

"I don't know. That is a big mystery to me. I told no one."

"Somebody must have known about the second box," Mary said with a sigh.

"Of course, Jeff did, and the director did. They may have assumed where I hid the second box."

"If Tyler was following you to this apartment, he was mugged by someone else, someone outside the group. Who would that be?"

"I have absolutely no clue. This is where this whole thing stinks. You get the feeling the plan was being deliberately exposed, like they wanted someone to steal it."

"Why?"

"I don't know. I don't know. I am so sorry about all this. I am so sorry." Bill rubbed his face with his hands.

"Who else in the US was part of this scheme?"

"Jeff Milbank, my boss, and Sam Kopitski, with Sebastian Corporation."

"Who was giving the orders?"

"I suspected someone in the US government was."

"The national security adviser, your former CEO?"

"I don't know."

"Anything else you want to tell us?"

"I am so sorry I was ever sucked into this. It is all about the black box. I don't know what it really is, how it works, and why they handled it so sloppily. I am still at a loss who instigated all the chatter that raised the red flags." Bill placed his head down into his hands.

"Okay, Bill. We are done with you for now, but you will remain in custody."

Bill Sorenson was escorted back to his holding cell. Mary looked at Natalie. "Any thoughts?"

"This gets crazier by the moment. You get the feeling the plan was designed for the black box to be hyped, discovered, and stolen. But why?"

"I need to call General Masoud and tell him about the interview. I will also bring our director up to speed. I need to call him now before the deputy calls me," Mary said.

59

GENERAL MASOUD FINISHED questioning Mounir Al Misri, Pinnacle's commercial director, when his cell phone buzzed. It was Mary. She told him about the Pinnacle board member. He said nothing. Mary knew that was disturbing for him to hear.

He finally told Mary, "I'll follow up on my end. My questioning of the commercial director did not reveal anything new or any involvement. Joseph Ferguson, the technical director, is next. I'll watch the interrogation and call you back." The general hung up and watched the interrogator do his work.

"Joseph, we have read your file. We have also been following your activities over the last few weeks, which includes all telephone calls from your office, your cell, and your apartment. What we found is very damning. Until this investigation is finished, you will surrender your passport. You are not allowed to leave the country. Is that clear?"

"Yes, sir, it is."

"You realize how serious this is for you. We expect you to answer all of my questions honestly, without any hesitation. Understood?"

"Yes, sir," Joseph replied.

"You have been working with Abdulla Amin, a board member of Pinnacle Enterprises. Correct?" the interrogator asked.

Joseph said nothing. He looked surprised, unsure of the question. "He is on our board. I talk to him from time to time, but I'm not sure what you mean by 'working with him.'"

"He directed you and gave you the orders regarding the server, the black box, right? Don't lie to me," the interrogator demanded.

"Yes," Joseph said with apparent resignation.

"Was your CEO, Mr. Khoury, part of the discussions?"

"No."

"What did Mr. Amin ask you to do?"

"He asked me to steal the black box from Mr. Grant's hotel room."

"Did he say why?"

"He said Mr. Grant was informed of the theft ahead of time."

"That was strange. Did you know why?"

"I was told Mr. Grant was part of the team."

"You attacked Mr. Grant in the apartment belonging to Mr. Sorenson. Why?"

"I was ordered to follow Mr. Grant. Mr. Amin told me he did not fully trust him, that there may be a duplicate black box."

"Did you find the second box?"

"No. When I arrived shortly after Mr. Grant, he had the apartment torn apart. He did not see me. I hit him on the back of the head before he turned. I thought I killed him. I left the apartment."

"What did you do to the first black box?"

Joseph was silent, hesitant.

"No lies. What did you do to the black box?"

"I sold it."

"Sold it! To whom?"

"To the Russians."

"How did you know how to approach them? Did Abdulla give you the contacts?" the interrogator asked. The general was listening; he did not expect this.

"Yes," Joseph said.

"Was it the Russian mafia?"

"Yes, it was the Russian mafia."

"Was that your idea?"

"No. It was Mr. Amin's."

"Did he say why?"

"No. I thought it was strange. He didn't tell me why."

"How much did they pay for the box?"

"They paid me five million dollars in cash. I gave it to Mr. Amin."

"Who else was involved or knew about this?"

"No one else that I know." Joseph's face was pleading.

"Anything else you want to tell us?"

"No, sir."

"Okay, Mr. Ferguson. You are under arrest until we decide what to do with you."

This was a new wrinkle. The Russian connection took a different turn. The general picked up his cell, called Mary, and told her about his interview.

60

CHAIRMAN MARWAN REQUESTED to join the general during the questioning of his CEO and the board member.

Elias Khoury, CEO of Pinnacle Enterprises, walked in, tall and dignified. He had an envelope in his hand, which he gave to his boss, Chairman of the Board Marwan Ahmed Marwan.

There was a letter inside, a letter of resignation. Mr. Marwan started reading the letter, slowly, calmly. "Elias, I accept your resignation. You know how painful this is for me. You were my trusted friend. From what Masoud tells me, you were not part of this treason, the only word I can use to describe it. Your crime, Elias, was amazingly poor judgment. You should never have allowed this fiasco to continue. You betrayed me and the company that honored you. Your punishment is loss of a prestigious position and banishment from Dubai. Publicly, you have resigned for health reasons."

"Abu Haidar, I have dishonored you and dishonored myself and my family. I can only say how sorry I am. I wish I could undo what I have done, but I can't. I was deceived. It is not an excuse, but I should have questioned things more rigorously. Please forgive me." He stood up and walked out of the room.

Abdulla Amin, the youngest member of the board of directors of Pinnacle, walked in. Expressionless. Unperturbed.

"Abdulla, serious charges have been brought against you. You know that." General Masoud looked at him with a combination of anger and contempt.

"Yes, I do," replied the defiant young board member.

"What you have done is treason."

"That is your opinion."

"How else would you describe it?" the general asked.

"I don't know what the charge is."

"Abdulla, I don't have time or patience for your arrogant games. I want truthful answers. Did you collaborate with Bill Sorenson to deceive the company about the nature of the recommended cyber-security?"

"I worked with Bill Sorenson but not to deceive anyone."

"Did you not work with Jeff Milbank on a plan to exchange the proposed server with a potential offensive weapon?"

"I worked with Mr. Milbank. I had no knowledge of an offensive weapon."

"Why were you working secretly with CTC?"

"I was ordered to." He shrugged.

"Ordered? Ordered by whom?"

"I cannot tell you."

"What do you mean you can't tell me? I am in charge here! I can place you in a cell right now if you refuse to answer."

"Abdulla, as it looks now, you are part of a treasonous plot that could land you in jail for a long time, with no rights, no more life in Dubai, disgrace to your family," the chairman said. "Do not make it worse for yourself. Think about the disgrace you will bring to your family. Your father is a friend of mine. I know how he will react. Answer General Masoud; you don't have an option."

"I was approached by Mr. Milbank of CTC and Mr. Kopitski of Sebastian Corporation about a month ago."

"Where?" the general asked.

"In Los Angeles, when I accompanied Mr. Khoury and others to look at STR's work."

"Anyone else go with you to meet them in Los Angeles?"

"No."

"Did you tell anyone?"

"No. Mr. Milbank and Mr. Kopitski told me they were working with our national security agency, as well as the US government. It was top secret. I was sworn to secrecy."

"Did you believe them?"

"Yes, I did. They were senior executives of major US companies."

"Did they tell you what the purpose of the plan was?"

"They told me it was a deterrent against aggression."

"Did they tell you how the plan worked?"

"No, they did not. I trusted them."

"Did they tell you which branch of the US government was involved?"

"They told me it was the CIA."

General Masoud and the chairman exchanged a puzzled look but kept silent.

"Abdulla, did you recruit Joseph Ferguson?" the general continued.

"No. He was recruited by Mr. Milbank, but I was asked to coordinate and direct his activities."

"Did Mr. Sorenson direct you?"

"My orders came directly from Mr. Milbank."

"Did you order Mr. Ferguson to steal the black box?"

"Yes."

"Why?"

"I was told by Mr. Milbank that we needed to protect it."

"Why? Didn't you think that was strange?"

"Yes, I did. I still don't know why."

"Did you sell it to the Russians?"

"Of course not."

"What did you do with the box?"

"I was told Joseph Ferguson kept it," the young director said, still defiant but unsure.

"What did you do with the five million?"

"What five million? I don't know anything about five million."

"Joe Ferguson said he gave you five million dollars."

"He is lying."

"Abdulla, don't lie to us. We have to have the truth," the chairman demanded.

"Abu Haider, I swear I am telling the truth," Abdulla Amin answered.

"Did you order the assassination of the two Russians?"

"No. I swear I did not." He started to look panicked.

"Who did?"

"I don't know. When I heard, I was totally shocked."

"Do you still believe what Mr. Milbank has been telling you?"

"I don't know. I don't know." He shook his head sadly.

"What exactly did you do for them?"

"I don't know. I thought I was helping my country and the Americans." Abdulla put his head down, the chip on the shoulder gone.

"Do you have anything to add to this mess? At least try to make some sense of this."

"I am so ashamed. So embarrassed. How could I be so stupid? Please forgive me, Abu Haider. Please do not tell my father, please." Abdulla started sobbing uncontrollably.

"You can go now. Do not discuss this with anyone. I will get back to you when we decide what we will do with you," the general said.

Abdullah, with his head down, still sobbing, left the room.

"Well, General, what are we going to do with this stupid, naïve boy? You know his family. It will be a major scandal."

"I agree. We have to come up with an appropriate punishment. At minimum, he helps us with getting the five million dollars and resigns from your board. And there will be one other punishment that is personal to him only."

"Let me work on that. Do you think the CIA may be behind this?"

"I don't know, but I will find out. I have to get back to Joe Ferguson and get to the bottom of this. We are not done," General Masoud said.

61

MARY WAS IN General Masoud's private office, waiting for him to finish his telephone conversation with his lieutenant. He had called her earlier and said it was urgent they meet.

"Joseph Ferguson has admitted to lying about the five million dollars he received from the Russians," the general told her as soon as he hung up. "He kept it. He was instructed to keep it until further notice. He claims the instructions were from Mr. Kopitski."

"Wait. I thought Milbank was giving the orders, not Sam Kopitski," Mary said.

"So did we. Apparently, the brains behind this is Sebastian Corporation. To what end, I have no idea. Mr. Ferguson may also be lying to cover for someone else." He exhaled. "Mary, this whole thing stinks. Abdulla Amin, the young director, was working with Milbank, thinking he was working with the US government and our national security. He was told this was a CIA-driven initiative. Mary, I demand to know if that is true. Is the CIA pulling the strings?"

"Masoud, I will be honest with you. I do not know, but I will find out. You have my word. One more thing: I think Joseph is lying. He must have the second box. There is no other explanation," Mary said.

"I thought the same thing. Let me follow up," Masoud said. He picked up his cell phone and called the captain. "Interrogate Joseph again about the box and also send a team to his home to search for it. It's urgent."

When he finished, Mary told Masoud, "I need to call my director immediately." Masoud understood and left the room.

Mary punched in the secure numbers for the director. He answered right away. "First, I am glad the architect is safe. We have Mr. Milbank and Mr. Kopitski under arrest, and there will be more. What is absolutely critical now is to retrieve the second box. It was a good thing the first one self-destructed. It must be found and brought back to us or destroyed," the director said.

"Yes, sir, understood. We are working on it as we speak," Mary said. When the director hung up, Mary left the room and found the general walking toward her.

"Mary, you were right. Ferguson confessed. He had the box in his home. I sent a team to go and bring it back here," the general said.

"General, have your team take it to the US Consulate and deliver it to Major Garfield." Mary said.

"Okay, I will."

62

"**MARY, ONE OTHER** thing has been bothering me. How did the assassin know where the Russians were holding the architect? And the exact timing? Somebody who knew all our moves must have arranged the assassination."

"Who do you suspect?" Mary asked.

"I'm beginning to believe it has to be somebody on your side who is tied to the Russians."

"My two team members are Natalie and Rusty. I can't imagine either one of them would betray us or work with the Russian mafia. I don't believe it," Mary said.

"You also have Major Garfield. But, tell me, how long have you known Natalie?" he asked.

"You don't really believe Natalie would be the one. No, I can't imagine that. I have known her a long time. In fact, she should have called me by now." She picked up her phone and dialed Natalie's cell number. There was no answer. She waited and tried again. Again, no answer. "Strange," Mary said aloud.

She tried Major Garfield's number, and he answered immediately. "Chuck, where is Natalie? I have been trying to reach her."

"She left with Rusty; he was driving."

"Did they say where they were going?" Mary asked.

"I don't know. I tried to call Rusty, but he didn't pick up."

Something is wrong, she thought. "What was he driving?" Mary asked.

"The white Toyota SUV."

Mary hung up and looked at General Masoud. He stood up. "Let's go to the war room and see if we can track them," she said.

63

RUSTY WAS DRIVING with Natalie in the passenger seat. "Okay, Rusty, what is it you wanted to show me that is so important?" Just then, her cell phone rang. It was Mary.

When she picked up her phone, Rusty pulled out his gun and aimed at her head. "Don't answer. Put down the cell phone now!" he demanded.

"What the hell, Rusty? What is going on? What are you doing?" Natalie asked.

"Just be quiet. You will know soon."

He drove the car to an industrial area, dominated by warehouses. He drove up to a warehouse with a tall garage door. He pulled out a remote garage door opener and pressed the button. Then he drove the SUV inside and closed the garage door.

He ordered Natalie to get out of the car, his gun aimed at her. Natalie got out. Rusty opened the trunk and removed a blanket that covered the black box. He pulled the box out and placed it on the floor, the gun still pointed at Natalie.

"Rusty, what are you doing? Whatever it is, you know you can't get away with this. If you are in some sort of trouble, this is no way to solve it. Talk to me, Rusty, talk to me."

"Be quiet, Natalie. You can't help. Nobody can."

"Talk to me. What have you done?" She was almost pleading.

"No, Natalie, it is too late. You can't help me. I am sorry I had to drag you into this. But you are my insurance."

"Insurance for what, Rusty? You will get caught. They will not let you get away, with or without me. Tell me what you have done. I can help you. I know I can," Natalie said.

Rusty kept looking at his watch. He was getting nervous and agitated. He was pacing, waving his gun, and constantly checking the time.

"Rusty, you are waiting for some people, aren't you? They want the box, right? You know they will kill you. They will kill us both. They have to; they can't leave witnesses. You have created a mess, Rusty. Trust me. I can help you. No matter what. You must share with me what you have done. We are running out of time."

Rusty stopped pacing. His demeanor changed, and he became almost calm. With his gun still aimed at Natalie, he asked her to sit down on an old chair in the warehouse. His eyes, Natalie noted, had transformed from showing agitation and fear into sadness, a calm sadness.

"Last year, the Russians approached me, offered me money. I needed money, gambling debt. They held the notes. They said they would forgive the notes and provide me more credit. All I had to do was let them know about any new cyber technology initiatives. That is all I was to provide. I was naïve and desperate, not realizing that by paying me the money, they owned me," Rusty said.

"Last week, I told them about the Dubai project and the server. They wanted to know all the details. There wasn't much to tell them. I held back on most of the sensitive activities. They were very keen, kept calling me for updates. Things changed with the kidnapping of Jennifer and then with Andy." Rusty stopped.

"So far, Rusty, what you have done is illegal, and you will be prosecuted for it. But it is manageable. We can work something out." Natalie tried to be reassuring.

"I know that, Natalie. I gave them the location of the house where Andy Sykes was held and where the two Russians were assassinated. It gave them time to position a professional assassin in place to kill the two," Rusty explained.

"Rusty, you don't know that. We think it was an Aeroflot pilot who may have been part of the mafia," Natalie said.

"No, Natalie. I know they did it. The pilot was an innocent victim. His body will be recovered someday, somewhere close to the building, if not inside it."

"Rusty, why did they want you to bring the box and me with you?"

"The box was an unanticipated prize. You, I don't know exactly why they wanted you. They told me you were an insurance policy. Natalie, I am sorry."

"Rusty, look at me. We can't stay here, waiting for them to get here and kill us. You know they will. Let's get in the car and leave. I will support you. Come on, Rusty, we are running out of time," Natalie begged.

"Okay, Natalie, let's go."

Natalie jumped in the car. Rusty picked up the black box, put it back in the trunk, and covered it with the blanket. He pressed the garage opener, and the door opened. Rusty jumped into the driver's seat and started driving away from the warehouse.

64

GENERAL MASOUD AND Mary were in the war room, looking intently at the screens. They watched the footage from the cameras surrounding the consulate. They saw the white SUV leave around the time the major said. The technicians were following its path.

They watched as the SUV entered a warehouse district, but the cameras lost track of it. The general ordered teams to mobilize and search for the vehicle.

However, footage from five minutes earlier showed the white SUV leaving a warehouse with two passengers in the front seat. Mary and Masoud watched it speed out of the warehouse. They saw a black SUV appear on the screen, speeding toward the white one.

General Masoud called his commander on the ground and gave him the instructions. Then he looked at Mary, who was watching the screens. "Our people are close by. We have our police helicopters in the air. They will spot them soon."

"General, make sure my two agents are not harmed. I don't know what the real story is yet. I don't want them hurt. I'll try calling Natalie again," Mary demanded.

"They will not be harmed. Is there anything you have not told me? There are too many moving parts, too many surprises."

"General, I have not kept anything from you. I am at a loss, as you are. I still believe this whole fiasco started as a rogue operation by our American companies that went wild. The execution was clumsy and unsophisticated; its intent was misguided, illegal, and dangerous, a toxic combination of greed and maybe ideology."

"I am puzzled about the potential Russian connection. Is Natalie a Russian agent? Are they after the box?" General Masoud was clearly frustrated.

Mary picked up her cell phone and called Natalie, who answered after a few rings. "Mary, listen, I will give you details later. I have convinced Rusty to give himself up. We are coming in. We are being chased by a black SUV, and they are gaining on us. No question of their intent. We need support ASAP."

"Okay, Natalie. I am here with the general. His forces are out to help you. They have been given instructions to protect you. Keep the line open."

65

NATALIE WAS WATCHING the black SUV gaining on them. Rusty hit the brake and skidded to a screeching stop. The road ahead was barricaded by police cars. The policemen had their guns drawn and aimed at them.

Natalie saw the black SUV turn around quickly and speed away, chased by a fleet of police cars. She looked at Rusty. He was staring straight ahead.

The officer in charge pulled out his loudspeaker. He was on the phone, most likely with General Masoud. "This is the Dubai police. Please step out of your vehicle with your hands up. You will not be harmed, orders from General Masoud. Get out of the car slowly with your hands up."

"Rusty, let's go. We will not be harmed. Rusty, we have to. We must go. Put your gun down. Let's go!" Natalie implored.

Rusty did not react. He just kept staring straight ahead.

"Rusty, please, let's go," she said more calmly.

"Natalie," Rusty said after a long pause. "Natalie, you leave. Leave now. Give me a few minutes. I need some more time. Then I will join you. I will. Now go."

Natalie stared at Rusty for a long time. She slapped him hard and then proceeded to open the door slowly. She got out with her hands up and started moving toward the police. She stopped and turned around, begging Rusty to join her without saying a word. Rusty looked at her and nodded knowingly.

Natalie continued walking until she reached the officer. She shook his hand and turned around, waving for Rusty to join her. There was no movement. The officer looked at Natalie and asked, "What should we do?" Natalie said to wait.

At that moment, they heard a loud boom, like an explosion from inside the white SUV, accompanied by a quick flash of light. The vehicle was completely destroyed.

Natalie shouted, "No, no . . . Rusty, no!" She knew. That was Rusty's way to end it, end the pain, the shame, the regret.

Natalie's phone rang; it was Mary. "Natalie, thank God you are safe. We saw what happened. Is Rusty dead?"

"I'm sure he is. The black box is destroyed with him," Natalie said.

"Natalie, come in now. The general and I will be waiting."

"What happened to the black SUV that was following us? Who was in it?"

"It crashed in a fiery shootout. Both people inside were killed. The police are investigating."

66

MARY WAS IN the secure room in the consulate, waiting for the director. She had finished questioning her witnesses and was pleased that Andy, Jennifer, and Natalie were safe. The events of the day had shaken her. Her discussion with General Masoud was disturbing. He demanded answers, and so did she.

"Hello, Mary." The CIA director's image came alive on the large screen. "I hope this dark episode is over. I am sorry to say this is not a bright spot for us. Give me your report, please."

"Well, sir, I prepared our report for you. It should get to your desk momentarily. As we suspected, this was a rogue operation that included senior executives of two American companies, CTC and Sebastian Corporation. They convinced Pinnacle Enterprises to include an advanced, untested cybersecurity system in their project. They had support from the office of our national security adviser. The program was also supported by the CEO of Pinnacle Enterprises. What was not shared with the group was that the real objective was the installation of an offensive cyber weapon in parallel with and under the cover of the development project. The weapon was based on the same technology as what was proposed and would be converted with modifications, when needed." She paused to let the information sink in.

"The assassination of the two Russians has changed our conclusion and turned it on its head," she continued. "We have discovered that a company board member and a senior staff member have been working with CTC, helping them advance their agenda. The most puzzling and disturbing news is the sale of the black box to the Russian mafia for five million dollars, knowing the mafia would sell it for a much higher price to the Russian government or the Iranians, the same groups we intended to harm in the first place. It does not make sense." She stopped again to emphasize the enormity of the situation.

"The UAE's internal security suspects the CIA or national security. They are convinced we have blood on our hands, sir. One of our agents turned out to be an informant, recruited by the Russians. He gave them the location of the house where the architect was held, giving the Russians time to place an assassin there to execute the two mafia men. Rusty, our agent, is dead; he killed himself." She felt a catch in her throat.

"What's more, internal security suspects that we have not been forthcoming. Sir, I don't mean to be disrespectful, but are we directly or indirectly responsible? Did we have a hand in this fiasco?" Mary asked her boss and mentor.

"Sir, I have to express to you my total disbelief. How can two highly sensitive and classified pieces of hardware of this kind be handled in such a careless, sloppy, and dangerous way? For that matter, how can this happen without the approval and support from the highest level?"

"Mary, you are not being disrespectful. You are doing your job, as you should. While you were uncovering the happenings in Dubai, we were doing the same here," the director of the CIA said.

"Let me start by telling you we absolutely had nothing to do with the assassinations. I am convinced none of the current players did either. There is no doubt it was carried out by others related to the Russians, more precisely the Russian mafia."

Mary let out a relieved sigh.

"Our people have interrogated the executives of the two companies, and what we found was surprising. Both boxes, the servers, were identical, planned as advanced servers for the Dubai project," the director said. "However, they were both altered. The first box was determined to be a sophisticated, state-of-the-art cybersecurity defensive weapon and would be highly prized by any country with its capability to become an offensive weapon and reverse cyberattacks." He paused before continuing.

"The second box, we believe, was also altered, but we don't know how. It was identical to the first, but not the lethal offensive weapon as the first. Both executives cannot explain how the box was altered or by whom."

"Who was behind this, sir?" Mary did not expect this. "Was it the national security adviser?"

"No Mary. I don't think so, but I am not certain. We have to be careful how we approach this. We need to continue our interrogations at both fronts until we get to the bottom of this."

She wasn't sure what to say. "We have a lot of loose ends and too many unknowns . What happens next? Who else is involved? How do we handle this with our UAE partners?"

"Well, as you have already figured out, this whole episode is highly volatile and has to be handled with extreme sensitivity. I have discussed the matter with the UAE minister. They do not want any publicity that would be harmful to both countries or used by our enemies. We agreed to have the matter dealt with discretely, with the same agreed-upon narratives. The two company executives have resigned. The two will face jail time, part of a confidential plea bargain because of national security. The explanation will be that the charges are for the misuse of funds." The director paused, seeming to consider this.

Considering the potential damage, I believe this to be our best option. Before we get back to our partners in the UAE, we have to have all the facts. We don't have much time," he said.

After a moment, he continued. "Mary, please brief General

Masoud. I am glad the Sykeses are unharmed. They seem to be a tough pair. See you back in Washington. We need you here; our cyber war is our highest priority against the relentless attacks. Before I close, let me assure you I am not and never have been involved. Are there others? There may be. Is anyone in the US government responsible for the assassination? I have to say, unequivocally, no." With that, the director ended the conversation.

Mary picked up her cell phone and called General Masoud to tell him about her conversation with the director. In turn, the general told her about the discussions he had with the defense minister and also Chairman Marwan. They both agreed to take care of loose ends.

Mary called Natalie and briefed her on her discussion with the director. She told Natalie they had to question three of the witnesses again. Too many unanswered questions.

67

JENNIFER, ANDY, AND Bob were invited to join the chairman of Pinnacle for lunch. Ayman and Hania, as well as Mary and General Masoud, were also there.

"Welcome," the chairman said with his usual dignity. "I want to thank you for your dedication, integrity, and courage. Unfortunately, Mr. Khoury will not be with us. Neither will Mr. Ferguson. We already have replacements for them. Mr. and Mrs. Sykes—"

"Andy and Jennifer, sir," Andy interrupted.

"Okay, Andy and Jennifer, but only if you call me Marwan. Well, Andy and Jennifer, this chapter is closed. I hope none of you are giving up. We have a big project to build."

"Are you kidding, Mr. Chairman? I mean, Marwan. We love it here. We are just getting started," Jennifer jumped in.

"Mr. Sykes, I have arranged for you and Mrs. Sykes to spend a few nights in our hotel in the desert. I guarantee you will enjoy the peace and quiet it offers. You need it before you get started on Al Bustan for us," Chairman Marwan Ahmed Marwan said to Andy Sykes, his star architect.

Mary stood up and said she needed to leave, tie up some loose ends before she left to the US. General Masoud said he would walk out with her.

"Mary, how can I help?" He said

"Thank you Masoud, what I have to do is circle back to a few people I need to interview them again. I will call you" Mary said as she left .

68

BACK IN HER office at Langley, Mary Tobias was reviewing the details of her presentation and summary for the director of the CIA. Natalie was assisting her with the report. They had arrived from Dubai an hour earlier and went directly to the CIA headquarters. Meeting with the director and his deputy was their most urgent priority.

"Do you have what you need?" Natalie asked.

"I think so," Mary answered.

"Did you share any of this with General Masoud?"

"No, I will after my meeting with the Director."

"Good luck Mary. I will be here waiting."

Mary picked up the folder, stood up and started towards the door. She stopped, looked at Natalie and said, "How do I look?"

"You look fine Mary, just fine," Natalie said, standing up and giving her a hug. Mary left her office.

She walked into the director's office. The director and Tim Patterson, his deputy, were seated, waiting for her final report and conclusions. The director stood up and motioned for her to sit on the chair by his table across from him and on the other end from his deputy.

"Mary, welcome back," the director said. "This has not been pleasant for any of us. We have been fortunate that we don't have the press to deal with. I spoke with the defense minister, and, as expected, he is not happy. I promised I will follow up with our findings after I hear what you have. Did you share your conclusions with General Masoud?"

"No sir, I told him I would after our meeting. I wanted your approval first," Mary replied as she took out the papers from the folder.

"Mary, you should have briefed me before you left Dubai as I instructed you," deputy Patterson said, reprimanding Mary. She said nothing.

"Since our last talk sir, my team and I spent our last day in Dubai reviewing the materials and questioning a few key witnesses for the second or third time. We had loose ends to fix and questions to be answered. I believe we have what we were missing." Mary waited for a response. There was none from the two men.

She continued. "We were operating under several wrong assumptions that led us to initial wrong directions. The first was we assumed the operation was a single track and a well-coordinated plan. It was not. Second, we assumed there were two highly classified boxes, known only to the executives of the two companies. That was not the case either. These assumed altered boxes were well known and sanctioned by this government—the US government. Finally, we assumed we were dealing with one altered server. We were not. Both servers were altered." Mary stopped, looking at her notes.

"This doesn't make sense Mary. Are you sure about all this?" the deputy asked.

"Yes, we are, Tim. Let me walk you through the whole thing. It will clear things up. The development of the two servers, altered from the original server, were approved by our national security advisor," Mary said.

"That's preposterous!" Tim said.

"Go ahead, Mary. Let's hear the rest," the director said.

"While the national security advisor authorized the alteration to advanced capabilities, he did not authorize and was not aware that the servers were transported to Dubai to be placed in the Al Bustan project," Mary said.

"The first duplicate made of the original server was altered to be a highly advanced and classified hardware. It had the capability to become an offensive weapon that can disable electronic functions. Jeff Milbank of CTC and Sam Kopitski of Sebastian Corporation concocted the scheme to place and test this server in the project. If successful, it would result in significant profits. They also assumed no repercussions from the US government," Mary continued.

"They shared their plan with Bill Sorenson, VP for CTC, who was in charge of implementation. They didn't have full confidence in Bill who had a reputation as a heavy drinker, but they didn't have a choice. They also recruited the young board member of the development company to be their on the ground local support without divulging details of the plan. They convinced Elias Khoury, the CEO of the company, to include the hardware in his project."

"Where's this going Mary? We already know all this," the deputy interrupted.

"Be patient Tim. I will get there," Mary said.

"The plan started to unravel when the security agencies raised the alarm of potential terror attack on the project. The architects were demanding access to the server and Bill Sorenson was getting nervous and hid the servers. He shared the location with Tyler Grant, the new architect with the firm, who Sorenson had promoted to be hired and recruited to help him. Unbeknownst to Bill, Grant was working with Jeff Milbank. He stole the server and hid it in his hotel room, as instructed by Milbank," Mary said.

"Did they have support from us, any of our agencies? "the director asked.

"Yes sir, they did," Mary replied.

"Who? What agency?"

"I will get to that shortly sir, if you allow me," Mary said. "The two executives working with a member of our national security, were unaware of an alternative plan being implemented. The plan was to alter the second server into another highly advanced cyber weapon, a weapon in many ways that was more effective. The server was programmed to be a trojan horse that was capable of introducing malware, undetected, of penetrating electronic networks. It can sit there and wait for the opportunity.

"The target of the initiative was Iran and how to place the server within the Iranian government network. The assumed terrorist buzz about potential attacks upon the project was orchestrated by the individual, not terrorists. The intent was to attract the attention of the Iranians that an offensive weapon is planned to be installed in the project, in Dubai, twenty kilometers from their border," Mary took a deep breath. The two men were listening, absorbing every word.

"The individual recruited two key players to implement the plan, Jason Bower, who assisted in placing the malware in the server that Sorenson had asked him to keep. The other was Joseph Ferguson, the technical director for pinnacle. He assisted in placing the online rumors, selling the server to the Russian mafia to turn around and sell it to Iran, unsuspecting the true nature of the server," Mary said.

"The plan fell apart when the Russians started following the architect and kidnapped his wife, assuming they needed the architect in unlocking the secret of the server and making it operational. The rest of the story is a plan that went out of control and resulted in the deaths of several mafia members—"

"Mary, this is a very serious charge against a member of our national security," the director interrupted. "You better have solid proof of your assumptions, do you?"

"Yes sir, I do." Mary stood up and handed the folder to the director. "I have the signed confessions of both MRs Bower and Fergusson. I'm confident both Mr. Milbank and Mr. Kopitski will confirm the identity of the individual initial participation, but the ignorance of the other scheme."

Mary looked at the director then at his deputy.

Tim Patterson stood up and, without saying a word, headed towards the door and opened it. He retreated back into the room as two US marshals walked in and handcuffed him.

"It was Mr. Patterson, your deputy sir, who was the mastermind behind this incredible fiasco," Mary said, continuing her stare at Tim. He returned the stare but said nothing.

"God only knows what the hell you were thinking or trying to accomplish. You are a disgrace," Mary said to Tim and sat down.

"Do you have anything to say Tim?" the director said.

Tim Patterson remained silent.

"Take him away, we will deal with him later," the director ordered the marshals.

He picked up the phone and gave the needed instructions. The US marshals escorted the handcuffed, but defiant Tim Patterson out of the office.

The room was silent, Mary waiting for her long-time mentor to speak. He stood up, went to the window, and gazed outside. He looked older, Mary thought.

"Mary, thank you for briefing me earlier so that I could have the marshals on standby. This has not been easy for you. You must know how much I appreciate it. I'll call the minister and let him know this was a rogue operation for commercial purposes and the perpetrators have been apprehended. You do the same with general Masoud. I don't want any reference to the hardware. It is classified."

"I don't understand what motivated Tim to do this, it doesn't make any sense," Mary said.

"I can't tell you what goes on in someone's mind. What I can tell you, knowing Tim, at least I thought I did, he is not motivated by money. This was some misplaced ideology and narcissism that drove him.

We'll try to figure it out," he said. "Mary, take a couple of days off. You deserve it."

"Thank you, sir. I will later," Mary said. "Right now we're dealing with a cyber-attack. Hackers have penetrated a major power company in Nevada, demanding ransom. We're working with the power company. She stood up, shook the director's hand, and left the room.

Made in the USA
Middletown, DE
21 December 2021

56768707R00144